MW00720388

THE
HONEST ATHEIST

"*The Honest Atheist* is funny. I mean, really funny. But that doesn't keep it from being deeply insightful! Thor is a great writer who blends apologetics and humor together like Mary Poppins' spoon-and-sugar thing. I highly recommend this book!"

—JARRET LEMASTER
Actor, producer at *The Babylon Bee*

"A unique blend of apologetics and comedy in a show biz plot you'll want to chase to the end."

—VICTORIA JACKSON
Comedian, actress, author, *Saturday Night Live* alum

"You've never read anything just like *The Honest Atheist*. It's a literary smoothie concocted of equal parts stand-up comedy, serious philosophy, Christian apologetics, Bible exposition, and great storytelling. See? I told you, nothing like it. You'll smirk over the humor. You'll lose track of time as the pages turn. You'll stop to revisit a paragraph you've just realized is deeply profound. You'll be jarred and offended a few times, too—but just enough to keep you honest in your thinking. Wow! This story's potential for good takes my breath away."

—JOHN KITCHEN
Author of *No Road Too Far*

"*The Honest Atheist* starts with a laugh and ends with a bang! Comedy meets apologetics in this hilarious and punchy novel from Thor Ramsey that is unlike anything I've read yet. If Bill Maher and Lee Strobel wrote a book together, I imagine it would turn out like

The Honest Atheist. Ramsey packs up-to-date arguments for faith in God, His creation of the world, and the atonement of Christ right next to a laugh on just about every page. This is not your typical case for Christ from a guy who is not your typical apologist. It will bolster the faith of believers, challenge the presuppositions of the skeptical, and provide comical food for thought to everyone—give it a read and see for yourself!"

—ERNIE BOWMAN
Author of *Legend of the Wapa*

THE
HONEST ATHEIST
THOR RAMSEY

Ambassador International
GREENVILLE, SOUTH CAROLINA & BELFAST, NORTHERN IRELAND

www.ambassador-international.com

THE HONEST ATHEIST

Hardcover ISBN: 978-1-64960-503-0
Paperback ISBN: 978-1-64960-645-7
eISBN: 978-1-64960-547-4

Cover design by Karen Slayne
Interior Typesetting by Dentelle Design
Editing by Sara Johnson

Scripture taken from The Holy Bible, English Standard Version. ESV® Text Edition: 2016. Copyright © 2001 by Crossway Bibles, a publishing ministry of Good News Publishers.

Ambassador International titles may be purchased in bulk for education, business, fundraising, or sales promotional use. For information, please email sales@emeraldhouse.com.

AMBASSADOR INTERNATIONAL
Emerald House
411 University Ridge, Suite B14
Greenville, SC 29601
United States
www.ambassador-international.com

AMBASSADOR BOOKS
The Mount
2 Woodstock Link
Belfast, BT6 8DD
Northern Ireland, United Kingdom
www.ambassadormedia.co.uk

The colophon is a trademark of Ambassador, a Christian publishing company.

To Marshall Allen,

who has always believed in me even though it's never paid off for him.

AUTHOR'S NOTE

Craig Kilborn is a real person who hosted *The Late Late Show* from 1999 to 2004. His role in this story is fictional, though, and I hope I have portrayed his fictional self to be as funny as his real self. The exchanges with Penn & Teller are based on actual events from my life (other than the murder investigation), and I did not embellish my dialogue with them unless it made me appear smarter. Likewise, I did meet Phyllis Diller in the green room of *The Late Late Show*, so that part is also true—the greenroom snacks *were* delicious. All descriptions of Las Vegas are accurate, and I stand by that. The hub of atheism *is* in Minneapolis, Minnesota. Everything else is purely fictional, as far as I can tell.

The publisher has asked me to warn you this novel has some shocking elements—as most satires do—but nothing that would cause Grandma to faint. (But don't let her read it standing up, just to be safe.) However, if you're extremely squeamish or have used the word "triggered" in a sentence without being ironic, then you may want to put this book down and move on. There's a nice series of Amish romances out there that you may prefer. Ideas have consequences, and any disturbing bits within these pages serve to enhance that reality.

CHAPTER 1

I first met Horton Murray when he worked for the *Los Angeles Times*, back when he was writing stories about things like clean comedians and the neglectful care of residents in old folks' homes and other such fare of social critics and cultural commentators. Though it must be stated that Horton Murray was never a conventional journalist. He received his Doctor of Philosophy degree from Harvard; but instead of teaching, he began writing articles, which led to a career in journalism and then to his bestselling book on atheism and his eventual departure from the *Los Angeles Times* when he didn't want to be told what to write anymore. He interviewed me, Sam Seitz, for his story about clean comedians because I happen to be one—an oddity now in the field of standup comedy, like dodo birds just before their extinction.

Horton Murray calls himself an "honest atheist" because he argues that nothing really matters since we came from nothing and will return to nothing. "Accidents don't have meaning," he says. "That's what an accident is by definition. It didn't mean to happen. How can something that didn't mean to happen have meaning?"

In 1997, he wrote a book called *The Honest Atheist,* which became an international bestseller. He is better known than I am, and I've been on *The Tonight Show* six times—a fact you'll hear me repeat whenever the opportunity arises.

Horton led the way for those who later came to be known as the New Atheists, but he has never considered himself a New Atheist—just an honest one. I once asked him, "Why are they called the New Atheists?"

"So as not to be confused with the Dead Atheists, who don't have agents," he said.

Horton was also quick-witted, another reason I liked him right away.

"What's the difference between the New Atheists and the Dead Atheists?"

"The Dead Atheists were socialists," he said. "The New Atheists are socialites."

Horton has never been one to season his words with salt, but he hit the talk show scene before suppression of speech was in vogue and varied forms of hypersensitivity destroyed dissenting opinions and civil discourse.

"The Dead Atheists understood the premise of atheism," he said with a grin. "But you know what really irritates me?"

I shot my eyebrows up as if to say, "Continue, please."

"The New Atheists have simply repackaged arguments made during the Enlightenment as if no one has ever heard them," he said. "Not an original bone in their brain."

As you can see, Horton isn't a fan of the New Atheists, even though he has been dubbed their leader. He once said, "Everyone's tall to intellectual Lilliputians." Maybe he was quoting someone. I don't know; I never asked. Horton has the philosophical oomph of the Dead Atheists with the sensibility of the New, though he would never admit it, which is why he is their predecessor in every sense. But he unwittingly created at least one Dead Atheist in my nephew Franky.

It would be difficult to measure how effective Horton Murray has been in destroying the faith of the faithful, if not for my fine-tuned faith-o-meter that measures his effectiveness with 100 percent accuracy. In this case, Horton succeeded beyond his wildest dreams with Franky, who from the beginning was visibly affected by Horton's influence—not that he shook or anything when Jesus was mentioned. It's just that when Franky opened his mouth, God didn't come out. Franky's tentative little candle of faith had been snuffed out by Horton's bestselling book on atheism. After his first year of college, Franky, who was homeschooled by his Christian parents so he wouldn't be soiled by the thinking of the world, informed them he no longer believed in God. (But he'd also become a vegan, so you take it in stride.)

In hindsight, I should have never introduced them. It turned out tragically for both. This is a crime story in one sense. But in a greater sense, the crime story is only background to the real story—that ideas have consequences, a truism most of us don't take time to consider because we're too busy living out ideas we don't even know we're influenced by.

"You ruined my nephew's faith," I said to Horton.

"What went right?" he joked.

"He read your book. No one's influenced my nephew more than you."

"I didn't write it to be influential. I wrote it because I felt it needed to be said."

"I must admit," I said, "I've always thought atheism is silly. If there is no God, then who are they angry at?"

"Not all atheists are angry," he said. "Just the ones who have book deals."

"You're funny. You should inject more humor into your books."

"Then no one would take me seriously."

"That *is* the problem with being a comedian."

"Don't worry," said Horton. "The angry atheists will soon be replaced by nice ones. They'll eventually cycle out."

"And what about the honest ones?"

"It just depends on what we're honest about. No one wants unadulterated honesty. If we step out of line and say what's not supposed to be said, they'll shut us up somehow. Who knows? Maybe they'll label us as right-wingers or something. That's always a career-killer."

"It's funny how the world functions like we're all still in high school."

He leaned his head back and nodded with his mouth open in that sad silent laughter motif.

Even with our opposing worldviews, or maybe because of them, Horton and I shared a common bond of nonconformity in this world. He was a minority swimming against the stream, living out the survival ethic he so dearly believed, not even pretending to find a meaningful way to live life in a meaningless universe. That's a remarkable mindset if you ask me. Still, he enjoyed a good magic show as much as the next person.

Though we were already acquainted with each other, Horton and I really became friends the night we were both in Las Vegas to interview the magic and comedy duo of Penn & Teller.

CHAPTER 2

Driving to Las Vegas from southern California only takes about three and a half hours and one speeding ticket. During my drive, I noticed the scenery was missing. That's really the only way to describe Nevada—a state that makes Arizona appear fertile. It's like the state gambled away all its cacti.

What's the best way to describe Las Vegas? Let's say you're driving down a dirt road at around twenty miles per hour. Sitting in the passenger seat next to you is a shapely young lady in an expensive little black nightdress, who opens her car door, jumps out, and rolls into the ditch. After she crawls out of the ditch—that's Las Vegas.

I was driving to Vegas, baby, Vegas to interview the atheist comedian-magicians Penn & Teller—not that they agreed to the interview. Being a good Christian, I thought I'd ambush them. Before I departed, I thought of placing a Jesus-fish eating a Darwin-fish on my bumper but decided against it since I didn't own one.

Penn & Teller's management told my literary agent they only do taped interviews—meaning something that's going to be on film or television. If only we were making a documentary. I told them my iPhone has a camera, and I have a YouTube account; but this didn't seem to impress them. My agent emailed them back and forth several times. I followed up with an email myself that shot for being cordial. The answer was still, "No thanks." We thought of saying I was a rock journalist with *Rolling Stone* magazine, who was doing a piece on celebrity atheists; but we thought this might be construed as lying, since none of it was true.

However, all was not lost. After every show, Penn & Teller had the habit of standing in the lobby to sign autographs, meet their fans, and have their pictures taken with people like mild-mannered Christians who offer them pocket Bibles. This was our chance. Our strategy was to wait until the line had nearly died down; and then, while I shook Penn's hand, my literary agent would take our photo while I subtly asked him a question or two.

Penn & Teller became nationally known in the late 1980s by appearing regularly on *The Late Show with David Letterman*, back when it was actually a late show. Penn is tall and husky, and Teller is short and impish. Penn talks a lot. Teller never talks. Their tricks are often fake-blood gory, flipping around chainsaws and swords, catching bullets in their teeth (maybe that's why Teller never speaks), doing the cups and balls trick with clear plastic cups, and the like. But they have always dressed dapperly, like two guys late for a wedding. They are both atheists. The one who talks, Penn Jillette, is an outspoken atheist—probably because of the talking thing. He even wrote a book about atheism called *God, No!* Penn has long, rippling black hair that looks like it could clutch you by the throat and make you sit down and shut up all by itself.

I made a note to self: *Proceed with caution during the interview.*

In the lobby of the hotel, I saw Horton Murray standing in line, checking in. He smiled and said, "The clean comedian," and shook my hand reservedly.

"I hate being called that," I said.

"Why? Because clean comedians aren't funny?"

"Brian Regan is funny."

"Yes, he is. The funniest."

"So, what are you doing here?" I asked him, hoping to change the subject from comedians who are funnier than I am.

"I'm going to interview Penn & Teller," he said.

When I told Horton that I also was in Vegas to interview Penn & Teller, he insisted I have the full Vegas experience.

"Let's go for one of the last Vegas meal deals: a thick steak for $5.99," he said.

At a casino, of course.

I texted my agent, Marshall: *I'm ditching you. See you at the show.*

The Ellis Island Casino is an odd name for a casino but accurate, nonetheless, because it appeared many of the patrons should have been quarantined—or at least given a separate room where they could blow smoke out of their nostrils without having to endure my California smoke-free look of disdain. Since the steak was only

$5.99, we decided to endure the cigarette smoke. The cleaning bill to get the smell out of my clothing was $9.98, but this wasn't a factor at the time.

Whatever the name of the restaurant at the Ellis Island Casino (I think it was called Restaurant), the decor was "deadheading back home because I can't get a load" truck-stop circa 1978.

Our conversation was polite in the beginning, even as we tripped around politics and religion, but then we started discussing our writing projects and seemed to accelerate to the familiarity of old friends.

"It's so good to talk to someone who doesn't agree with me," he said.

"That's normal for me," I said.

"Unfortunately, the people who surround me with themselves are generally . . . well—"

"Groupies?"

He chuckled and said, "Unfortunately." But that's never the goal of a comedian. We go for belly laughs, not polite chuckles.

"This has been quite enjoyable," he said. "I don't usually do this— dine with just one person."

"You might be the first atheist I've met who has groupies," I said.

"There's Penn & Teller."

"Still, you came first. I feel privileged, then, to dine with you." I held up my glass of water. "Here's to dissenting opinions," I said, and we toasted.

As our friendship developed, I began to realize Horton Murray didn't have many friends. The truth is that he kept everyone at a distance because of his bleak view of life. He had no serious romantic relationships. Everything was intentionally casual. But right away, for some reason, he felt at ease around me. I honestly don't know why because I wasn't particularly sensitive to his personality. He was very different that night we had dinner, compared to the time he had interviewed me for the *Los Angeles Times* when his demeanor was professional and detached.

Then the waitress plopped our plates in front of us and scattered the rest of that conversation into the clouds of smoke over our heads. The steaks were piping hot and without any seasoning—just the right amount of blandness. And after a thirty-minute wait, it turns out they were $6.99.

Welcome to Vegas, baby, Vegas.

CHAPTER 3

Penn & Teller's theater was at the Rio—a stark contrast to the Ellis Island Casino and their $6.99 steaks. The difference between the Rio and the establishment where we acquired our recent gastrointestinal difficulties can be best described this way: the girl sitting in the passenger seat never jumps out of the car. The theater seats were comfortable and velvety red, filled to 70 percent capacity on a weeknight. While perusing the program, I noticed under the "Thank You" section they listed Mac King, a comedy-magician whom I worked with years ago. I should have called Mac King. Maybe he could have arranged the interview. Secretly, I was hoping to go along with Horton for his.

The lights blinked—theater sign language for "the show's about to begin."

In his "This I Believe" segment for National Public Radio, Penn described his atheism as informing every moment of his life. It certainly informed the show in Vegas that night. Several times Penn said things like, "All miracles are a hoax, a fabrication, a trick by liars and cheats and swindlers. And I know them all."[1]

---

1   Penn & Teller live at the Rio, Las Vegas, 2015 (or thereabouts).

In this type of anti-supernaturalist worldview, anything seen to violate the laws of nature would be considered a miracle. Penn's hair, for example.

During one trick, Teller held up a rose petal, its long shadow clearly seen in the background. When he cut the shadow of the rose petal, the actual rose petal fell off. Horton leaned over and whispered to me, "Either something miraculous happened, or I just witnessed a great trick."

"Miracles don't cost $45.00 per person," I said.

"Are you not familiar with TBN?" he asked.

He made me laugh.

"Bull's-eye," I said. "But Penn & Teller's worldview doesn't allow for miracles."

"No. It doesn't."

"That's circular reasoning. They don't believe in miracles because their worldview says not to."

"All beliefs are circular in nature," he said, which prompted several questions within me, but I let him finish. "The truth is, we all approach our worldviews with preconceived notions—the circuit of our reasoning must start somewhere. It's not arbitrary. No one does a card trick with a blank deck. Even Penn & Teller will tell you that," he said. "I assume."

"All beliefs? Really?"

"I only believe what can be proven. And why is that?" he asked himself. "Because I have a scientific worldview."

"Watch out for your behind because you just circled around," I said.

"See? Circular."

I said very softly, "One cannot ever really know anything for sure."

"And why is that?

"I don't know for sure."

"Okay, go get in line with the agnostics," he said, and I laughed.

"I like this game," I said.

"Okay, then," he said. "I only believe what is completely reasonable to believe."

"Because you believe in reason."

"See? All belief systems are circular in nature."

"Even atheism?"

"I do not believe God is there. And why is that?" he asked me.

"Because you . . . have not seen Him there?"

"Now you got it."

"Somewhere, there is an atheist with a dog chasing its tail," I said, and he laughed this time. Comedians are in the habit of noting how many times people laugh at something they say, even during casual conversation. You never know what might be transferable to your act.

"The reality is that we all begin with premises," he said. "Then you begin to build your beliefs upon your premise, which is why your beliefs naturally lead back to your premise."

"Is that in your book?"

"You didn't read my book?" he asked, with a fake expression of hurt.

"Shhh. We shouldn't talk during the show," I said and looked back down from our balcony seats at the stage below us.

This was the kicker to me, though. In my mind, the live tricks Penn & Teller performed that night in Las Vegas paled in comparison to even reading about the miracles attributed to Jesus in the Gospels. When the report about a miracle is more engaging than a live magic trick, well, that says something about the miracle.

Maybe church should have a cover charge. Say, $45.00?

CHAPTER 4

When the show was over, we headed to our interview. Well, his interview. Horton was escorted backstage, as Penn & Teller are regularly courted by famous atheists. I got in line with all their fans. Horton didn't invite me to go with him because he thought my ambush interview would make a funnier story.

"Thanks for nothing," I said.

"If you're any good, you'll get an interview," he said.

I stood in the very back of the line in the off chance my interview went really well, not wanting to hold things up. I also wanted to delay the possible disappointment if Penn just rolled his eyes at me. This had been a long day already. Most people are not willing to risk being blown off, but I planted myself in line with some sort of Martin Luther complex: "Here I stand."

After watching Penn banter and patiently pose for pictures with dozens of fans, I finally stood before him and said, "Can I ask you a question?"

"Okay," he said.

"In your opinion, what's the most positive thing atheism has brought to the world?"

From the outset, he seemed a little prickly with me, maybe because he'd already declined to be interviewed by me. Twice. Maybe because I interviewed him, anyway. Maybe because my agent decided to stand behind me feverishly taking notes on his notepad instead of flipping on his tape recorder.

Penn Jillette stands six feet six inches tall with all the twitches of a charging bull who's been hooked by a matador. In short, he's intimidating. I am six feet, according to my driver's license; five eleven when I tell the truth about my height; and possibly six inches from nose to ground after this interview.

He stepped back, looked down at me (his only option), and said loud enough for the few people remaining to hear, "DNA." I thought that was it, end of ambush interview. Then he continued, still slightly perturbed, "Yeah, DNA will save the world. There's also Norman Borlaug, who was responsible for saving over fifty million lives, the most people saved by anyone." I couldn't assume this was a subtle jab at Jesus because Penn didn't know me from Adam.

He continued, "Richard Feynman. Darwin. Seventy percent of Nobel Prize winners since its inception. How many more do you want? The list goes on."

At this point, he was backing away, ready to use his Sharpie to sign someone's program or maybe warn Teller by tagging my forehead with a large checkmark.

Teller, the silent half of the duo, was not only signing autographs, he was also talking to people. With his voice. The man talks. I had mixed emotions about him breaking character. Did Harpo Marx talk in public? I never even imagined I would have a chance to interview Teller.

The crowd around Teller had dissipated, so I walked over and shook his hand while asking, "Out of curiosity, are you an atheist, too?"

"Of course," he said, as if to say, "Who isn't an atheist?" or "What else could I be and hang out with Penn? Have you seen that guy? He's intimidating. His curls alone could beat me unconscious."

Then I asked him the same question. "What's the most positive contribution atheism has made to the world?"

"Well, atheism is just a subset of objectivism. And objectivism is responsible for everything that is good."

Yes, this from a Las Vegas showman. Not the kind of erudition one would expect.

Teller seemed open to more questions, so I asked him, "What's the most negative thing atheism has brought to the world?"

He said, "Nothing."

Nothing? There seemed to be an emotionally motivated denial in such an answer, but I let it go. I guess nothing fools you better than the lie you tell yourself, which I think Teller himself said in a legitimate interview somewhere. Anyway, he continued, "But theism is responsible for a lot of bad stuff. Whenever you involve gods, bad things happen."

This is something I've noticed from being around many atheists, thanks to Horton Murray—they used the word "gods" instead of saying "God." I can only assume this is because the term "gods" is more generic and because polytheism (the belief in multiple gods) was discredited eons ago. If atheists used the word "God," we would all know Who they're talking about; and it's not their goal to give credit where credit is due.

"Okay, tell me this," I said. "If you could recommend only one book by an atheist, what would it be?"

"Anything by Ayn Rand," he said, which really surprised me. That same week, I was in the middle of a book called *The Age of American Unreason* by freethinking skeptic and Pulitzer Prize finalist, Susan Jacoby. Jacoby seemed rather dismissive of Rand when she wrote, "Forgotten in their original form but not gone, the worst pseudoscientific ideas emanating from the late nineteenth century are constantly being marketed under new brand names in the United States. Social Darwinism has never died: it manifested itself as a bulwark of eugenics until the Second World War; in the tedious midcentury 'objectivist' philosophy of Ayn Rand."[2]

Now, I'm no New York intellectual (probably because of the time difference), but that seems rather negative to me.

It was at this point that Teller, who was very mild-mannered and seemed legitimately interested in what people had to say, complimented me on my choice of eyewear.

"Those are cool glasses," he said.

"Thank you. Oliver Peoples."

At last, common ground between atheists and Christians.

I was just about to ask him the same two questions regarding Christianity when he noticed Marshall, my agent, writing speedily on his notepad. We had a little tape recorder, but it's not polite to record people without their consent. So, Marshall thought he would just write everything down in front of them.

"Who are you guys?" asked Teller.

---

2   Susan Jacoby, *The Age of American Unreason* (New York: Penguin Random House, 2009).

Penn just happened to be walking by at that moment, probably heading to his interview with Horton, and he said to me, "Hey, your modifier is in the wrong place."

He could see the confusion on my face, so he clarified, "That photo of the nuns on your website."

On my website, there was a black and white photo (I don't recall where I came across it) of ten nuns holding shotguns. The caption read, "Much to their surprise, the virgins awaiting Muslims in Heaven were not quite what they expected." The sentence is grammatically incorrect because the word "their" is modifying the word "virgins" instead of "Muslims." Bad grammar annoys me, too, but I give punchlines creative license. (Okay, let's be honest—I give all my writing creative license.) Whoever wrote that should have just dropped the words "much to their surprise," and the sentence would have been fine. But if that's the worst thing Penn could say about my website, I was okay with that. Still, I resolved to delete it or at least footnote his keen eye for grammar. God is in the details, after all. (And even though Einstein said that, he didn't believe in God as a Personal Entity, so let's stop using him like he was a champion of theism.)

"Oh," I said, surprised Penn Jillette would actually notice a grammatical error on my website. Maybe his crack about who saved the most people in the world *was* intentional. That's amazing. I think I was just mocked by Penn Jillette. How many Christians can say that? Oh, right. All of us. But mine was *personal*, so there.

"You gotta watch that," he said while walking backward.

"God doesn't exist, but that's no reason for bad grammar," I said jokingly because, you know, comedy.

"There might be hope for you yet," he said.

Following his remark, like all good Las Vegas showmen, both Penn & Teller disappeared. Marshall and I stared at each other, taking in the moment as the last two fans standing in the lobby. That's right—by this time, we were fans.

"He checked out my website," I said, my egotism unbecoming as always.

"Well, that explains why they declined the interview," said Marshall.

Everyone's a comedian.

CHAPTER 5

Like most people walking to their hotel after a Las Vegas comedy and magic show, our thoughts turned to objectivism—the philosophy created by Ayn Rand and disseminated through her extra-thick novels. When I saw Horton in the hotel lobby, I asked him, "So, how did your interview go?"

"They're fun and smart."

Since Horton was the smartest person I knew—or at least the most accessible one at the time, being that I didn't have to wait in line to talk to him—I went ahead and asked, "Did objectivism come up?"

"Objectivism?" he asked, adding some choice profanity to further express his feelings about the subject.

"Yeah, that," I said, not knowing much about it.

"Ayn Rand. She's discount Nietzsche."

"I know. I hate that about her," I said with mock frustration. "What's her philosophy again?"

"Take Nietzsche; remove his wit. Voilà. Ayn Rand. Some philosopher from Gettysburg College said as much. She taught a type of radical individualism, very much in line with the expressive individualism of our day. Let me guess. Teller brought it up."

"See? You should have included me in your interview," I said.

"I take it you got an interview then?

"You can read all about it in my book."

"What are you gonna call it? Your humor book on atheism?"

"I thought I'd just have a blank cover," I said. "Then in tiny print on the inside—*Glory to Nothing: The Comical Nature of Unbelief.*"

"The White Album of humor books," he said.

"Sure. I'll take that."

"You guys up for a late bite?" he asked.

"I'm always up for a bite," I said. "Marshall?"

Marshall nodded.

"Anything in mind?" I asked him.

Horton did have something in mind, which included pool tables; so the three of us drove over to the Las Vegas Cue Club for some chicken wings and billiards. It was only about ten minutes away, so we took the back streets—Desert Inn to Paradise.

The place still had a 1964 Rat Pack vibe with an overhang off the roof in a row of triangles—basically three small *M* roofs strung together. When we walked into the place, I half-expected to see Dean and Sammy playing Eight Ball at one of the tables.

Not even five minutes after ordering our wings, some twiggy-thin, twenty-something guy wearing Levis and a navy t-shirt sauntered over and asked us if we wanted to play a game of pool. As novices, we all just looked at each other.

"For money?" I finally asked.

"Doesn't have to be a lot," he said. "I'm a regular. It's a slow night. Just want to keep my edge. I tell you what, I'll spot you two balls.

You can play as a team if you want. And I'll even use whatever object you choose as my cue stick. But it can't be paper."

"What about a book?" asked Horton.

"Sure. I'll use a book," said the pool shark.

"You're gonna play pool for money using a book as your stick?" I clarified.

"Sure," he said.

Horton looked at Marshall and me. "I'm going to get my book. I gotta see this," he said as he jumped up and ran out to the car.

"So, how much are we playing for?" I asked.

"Let's play for seventy-five bucks—between the three of you. We'll play race to three. That's the first one to win three games in a row."

"That good with you, Marshall?"

He nodded.

"Deal," I said. "What's your name, by the way?"

"Lenny 'the Mop' Evans."

"The Mop?"

"Yeah, first time I used something other than a pool stick was a mop. Ever since, they call me Lenny 'the Mop.'"

"I'm Sam 'the Ham,' and this is Marshall 'the Mute.'"

We all shook hands.

"And this is Horton . . . 'the Uncertain,'" I said as he jogged back to the table.

"Uncertain?" asked Horton.

"Atheist doesn't rhyme," I said.

"And uncertain does?"

"Okay," I said. "This is Horton 'the Gorton.' Meet Lenny 'the Mop.' This game's gonna cost you twenty-five bucks, by the way."

"It's worth it just to see someone play pool with a book," said Horton.

Then he handed the book to Lenny, who looked at the cover and said, "No way! *The Honest Atheist?* You're Horton Murray?"

"I am."

"This book changed my life."

"How so?"

"Let's just say my occupation is, well . . . under the table. Illegal to some, like my wife. She used to struggle with how she felt about it. I'm not mobster-related or anything like that. It's just a living. I do it so I can spend more time playing pool, mostly. Anyway, she worried about it—lots. But then I gave her your book, and now she sleeps like a baby. Your book saved my marriage, really. And we're going on year number two."

"Congratulations," I said, and then I naïvely asked, "what's your occupation?"

He just lowered his eyes and frowned at me with an expression that told me I couldn't be serious, so I left it at that because I was about to experience the hush-hush occupation of Lenny "the Mop" Evans.

CHAPTER 6

"So, cue ball rule," said Lenny. "If you pocket it, take the shot behind the head string."

Marshall and I looked at each other hoping that would never occur; otherwise, we would have to ask what the head string was.

"And you're still spotting us two balls?" I asked.

Lenny nodded and began racking the balls like he was gathering up a group of old friends to share a joke. Then Lenny "the Mop" handed a stick to Marshall, who took his spot behind the cue ball. He revved his stick back and forth a little too long, then hauled back and violently topped the ball, rolling it mere inches.

We all laughed.

"That's like a long set-up to a weak punchline," I said.

"Do over," said Lenny the Mop.

Marshall repositioned himself, shot again, and actually hit the balls this time, even knocking one in.

"Okay," said Lenny. "You're solids, and I'm spotting you two balls. You pick."

Marshall pointed to two solid balls, and Lenny pulled them from the table, saying, "Still your shot."

Marshall looked at us helplessly, so I took the stick and chalked it like I knew what I was doing.

"Five ball in the corner pocket," I said. Then without giving it much thought, I popped the cue ball, which then tapped the side of the orange five ball; and it rolled in making that dampened thud, always a sound of emotional victory.

"Nice shot," said Lenny the Mop.

"Thanks." Then I realized, "We only have three balls left."

"Table's still yours," said Lenny, but I couldn't get a handle on his angle because he truly seemed to be encouraging me. What was I missing? I'll tell you what I was missing—the two ball in the side pocket.

"I'm up," said Lenny.

"This doesn't seem like a fair match," said Horton.

"That's the point," said Lenny, who then used the top edge of the spine from Horton's hardcover book to knock in one ball after another until he cleared the table in less than five minutes.

"That's game one," said Lenny.

"I think you scammed us," I said to him.

"I didn't," he said. "I offered to play you shooting with something other than a cue stick. How's that a scam?"

"Because you knew you could beat us."

"I haven't won three games yet," said Lenny.

"But you know you will," I said.

"Yeah, I do. But that's not a scam."

"The scam was the novelty," said Horton. "Offering to play with something other than a cue stick."

"That's not it," said Lenny.

"Then what is it?" I asked.

"Your desire to see it done," said Lenny. "I can always get newbies into a game with that angle. Besides, what would it matter if I did scam you guys?"

Horton shot his eyebrow up at me. "He has a point."

"What about the 'do whatever you want as long as you don't hurt anyone' line of thinking?" I asked Horton.

"It's a false measure," he said.

"It is?"

"It's so utterly subjective that it becomes a useless and immeasurable standard."

"Just stick with false," I said.

"I can claim that watching porn in the privacy of my own home is not harming anyone, but—"

"Stop. *Please.* You just psychologically scarred me."

"See? I would have never thought that sentence could be harmful," said Horton, "but I don't get to define harm. No one does."

"So that's the subjective nature of it?"

"Yes."

"The moral of the story," I said. "Never buy a used recliner."

I got a laugh with that one.

Marshall just wrote down, "Ha ha."

That's when our short and wide waitress arrived with our wings and a pitcher of water, surrounded by four empty plastic red cups; so Horton grabbed a cup off the tray, handed it to Lenny, and said, "Try this, Mop."

"It's *the* Mop," I said.

"Guys," said Lenny, "I've enjoyed listening to your conversation so much that I almost feel bad about taking your money."

"You haven't won yet," I said.

Then he used his plastic red glass to break the triangle of balls. He potted a solid, advanced us two balls, and then cleared the table again. It took him closer to ten minutes this time, but we were just as mesmerized by his skill.

"This is like Pascal's wager come to life," I said.

"Pascal's wager," said Lenny. "Is that the idea you should believe in God just in case He exists? You know, hedge your bets?"

"No," I said. "It's about being all in on what you think is true. You're betting your life that your view of things is right. That's Pascal's wager."

"Kind of like being a Charger's fan," said Horton.

After hearing this, I had to reiterate: "You're a Charger fan?"

"What are you doing next Sunday?"

"Don't tell me you're inviting me to a game?"

"Box seats," he said.

"Oh, you vex me," I lamented in my best Shakespearean accent. "I'm afraid I have my niece's wedding that weekend."

"Oh, well," he said. "Another time."

"Man, this has been great," said Lenny. "What I wouldn't give . . ."

Then he went on to smoke us in one last game of pool, using the waitress' pencil to clear the table. We all had the sense we were in the presence of greatness. I knew one day, I'd hear the name of Lenny "the Mop" Evans again.

CHAPTER 7

Things got ugly at my niece's wedding, and it had nothing to do with the bridesmaids' dresses. My niece, a committed, evangelical Christian, had one of those devout Christian weddings where the preacher referenced the infinite circle of the rings to remind the couple what was in store for them—not that they'll actually be married for all eternity. It will only seem that way. *Bada-bing.* (Look, I'm not cynical about marriage. I'm cynical about people's romanticized views of marriage. "'Til death do us part" itself seems a little cynical. What's the goal of marriage? *Death.*) Then the preacher quoted 1 Corinthians 13 (misunderstanding the context) and finally had to assist the couple in lighting a stubborn unity candle. Thankfully, at the reception, the groom washed the bride's feet, forgoing that creepy tradition of removing her garter in front of elderly people and baffled children.

Franky brought his atheist girlfriend to the wedding, who exploded one of the great modern myths about atheists—that they're all smart. Not all atheists are smart. Smart people are smart. Some smart people believe in God, and some don't; but not all atheists are smart people.

During the wedding festivities, Franky's date, Syd Hawkins, was deeply offended—first, by the overtly Christian wedding and second, by a toast given by the newly married couple's grandpa, my dad, whom I've always called Pop. While toasting the happy couple, Pop commended my niece on her desire to start a family rather than pursue a career. I'm aware this might offend many women, but most of them weren't at the wedding. This young atheist woman left everyone a lasting wedding memory by approaching Pop and giving him the what-for with a heavy dose of expletives.

My niece, wanting to defend her grandpa, said to Miss Hawkins, "You're entitled to your opinion," which really isn't theologically correct because if truth is truth, then no one's entitled to their opinion. We can hold opinions, but they won't matter in the long run, if you know what I mean.

Syd ranted about how dumb Pop's opinions were in a way that made it apparent she had spent the last hour sitting at the bar. (There was a restaurant next door. You have to be very careful about picking venues, my friends.)

Pop asked her what she based all her opinions on.

She slurred, "Knowledge."

"Out of all the knowledge in the world," said Pop, "how much do you think you possess yourself?"

She claimed 90 percent. Being very young and very drunk, she may have felt like a genius; but the rest of the conversation testified against her. But there you have it: she claimed to possess 90 percent of the knowledge in the world.

Pop said kindly, "That's an awful lot of knowledge."

She was being set up, of course; and being drunk, she took the bait, not realizing she was speaking to a man who wrote bestselling books on Christian apologetics.

Pop asked her, "What year did King Henry V reign?"

She was off by several hundred years. (I only know that because he gave her the answer. I don't need alcohol to be stupid.) Then he asked her several similar questions she didn't know the answers to either. She compensated with a string of vulgarities, shouting loudly and proudly. She did possess 90 percent of the world's cuss words.

My wife heard every word while feeding our baby in the lady's room. Having had enough, my wife walked out and said to her nephew's girlfriend (I had disowned him at this point), "What are you thinking? This is someone's wedding day."

With both her arms outstretched, the drunk girl lunged at my wife, who was holding our baby. I don't think Syd Hawkins, soused assailant, thought her attack through very well. Was she going to choke my wife or beat her over the head with our baby? Even teenage gang members know it's not cool to attack a woman who's holding a baby—I hope. Franky snagged his date by the back of her shirt and held her back, saving my wife from the ranting wildebeest he had brought to the wedding. Slapping away Franky's grip, Syd stormed off to the women's room and ranted at the echoey walls.

Franky looked at me apologetically and said, "She's pretty nice when she's not drunk."

"How often is that?"

"Yup, yeah," he said. "Not enough."

Like the tie pinching his neck, Franky was uncomfortable in his own skin. Even at twenty-one, with a Poindexter haircut; his funky, checkered cotton shirts; and a belt too high on his pants, he looked like a kid who should be advertising erector sets—always studious, a born waterboy. Both he and Dinika had matured before my eyes in the same home, the oldest and the youngest. While the youngest honored her parents with her Christ-centered wedding, the oldest brought a date who denied the very existence of everything the wedding celebrated.

We could hear Syd barfing in the women's room.

I said to Franky, "You got a moment?"

CHAPTER 8

With his date preoccupied, I put my hand on Franky's shoulder and bobbed my head for him to follow me to an outdoor patio that was relatively empty with most of the festivities happening inside.

"Okay," I said. "I'm not going to persuade you or debate you or argue you back into the faith . . . I just want to understand. Tell me how you became an atheist."

I wanted to get the lowdown on his defection from believing God is there to believing He isn't because this kid used to spend the night in our home, go to the movies with us, and play putt-putt golf on our dime. *Was it something we said?*

Franky was open about his transition from confused evangelical teenager to assured militant atheist. During his teenage years, he became less dogmatic about Christianity: "There were many things about the Bible that I didn't believe on a moral level," he explained. "Sinning is bad, but I didn't know if anyone could tell who was going to Hell and who wasn't."

"I have the list if you'd like me to send it to you."

"If it was only that simple," he said. "It's too hard to judge behavior. It was always a drag, wondering, 'How do I know if God isn't going to be mad that I'm smoking or swearing?'"

Franky was the son of my sister, Abigail, and her husband, Andy—globetrotting Christian recording artists. Even though he grew up in an evangelical Christian home, he seemed to have little or no understanding of the Gospel. His view of Christianity was the ever-popular "moralistic therapeutic deism," where God is primarily concerned we act like good little boys and girls. It was about behaving a certain way to secure the favor of God and gain admittance to Heaven. There's nothing of the Gospel of grace in that understanding. It's a widespread but tragic misconception, propagated by well-meaning youth pastors who end up teaching kids more about dodgeball than regeneration and justification— not that there isn't a place in church for concussions and bloody noses. I just prefer they happen in the board meetings, as usual.

Besides his moral qualms, Franky said the cracks in his already fragile beliefs about Christianity were mostly scientific in nature, beginning with creationism: Adam and Eve, the earth being six thousand years old, and a guy named Ken Ham who some people mistakenly believe is in prison for teaching Christians they don't have to pay their taxes. This is inaccurate. It's another young earth creationist by the name of Ken Hovind who is in prison for not paying taxes. He was sentenced to six thousand years, I think.

Upon graduating as valedictorian with perfect attendance (he was homeschooled), he started reading up on science, trying to catch up with the indoctrination of his public-school peers.

He said, "I didn't feel like I learned a lot about science," which is odd because I went to a private, secular boarding school and feel the same way.

Whereas Franky may blame his mother's lack of scientific credentials, I can only blame prom for mine. Prom was fun. We decorated for it during science class. I guess there are drawbacks to both homeschooling and private boarding schools.

In his search to catch up, he came across a book called *Black Holes and Time Warps* by Kip S. Thorne, who was a student of Stephen Hawking.

"Personally," I said, "I'm a little amazed anyone could be influenced by a scientist named Kip."

Franky said, "Yes, well, evolution is always brought up because it's the standardized theory of how we came to be."

Then he told me he read *The Blind Watchmaker* by Richard Dawkins and *Defeating Darwinism* by Phillip Johnson, which isn't a fair fight at all. Johnson's book is nearly written at a child's level, while Dawkins' book is for emotionally immature adults. Okay, I guess that is a fair fight. Johnson has another book written for adults with a thesis that interacts well with Darwinists called *Darwin On Trial*. But if you want to read a really good book on the issue, I recommend one by my second favorite atheist, Thomas Nagel. It's called *Mind & Cosmos: Why the Materialist Neo-Darwinian Conception of Nature is Almost Certainly False*. Enough said.

Franky added, "Science was not pointing toward creationism."

In his mind, the idea of Christianity became weaker and weaker as he explored its logic. Soon, he had to admit his faith was hanging not only by a thread but by one that was merely clinging to the material of his shirt. All he had to do was pick it off his sleeve like a piece of lint, and voilà, he discarded Jesus like so many dust bunnies.

"Josephus was a fraud," he said. "Christianity's moral code didn't make sense, either. As a person who tries to be logical and straightforward about things, I didn't see enough evidence. It was really, really scary at first. Pascal's wager, you know, that sort of thing. But what if I was raised Muslim, then would I be in the same situation? At about nineteen, I said to myself, *I can't really do this anymore with a good conscience. I can't say that I approve of these messages.* Prayer felt more and more futile."

Prayer and disbelief in God are never a good mix, but I wondered to myself, *Is evidence the real issue?*

"I call myself an atheist," he said, "because I don't believe anything without proof. And there just isn't any evidence of God in the world. The problem with the whole thing . . . evidence. That is the problem to me."

"What kind of evidence do you think you need?" I asked.

"This would make me believe in God: if God is all-powerful, all-knowing, and wanted His will to be known, there could be . . . well, if the Bible had predictions that were recorded as truth . . . like if Jesus had said, 'There's this place that's going to be called New York City, and I've signed my name under the corner slab of cement at Forty-second and Broadway. Look for it someday after it's created, and that will be your proof.' That might do it. He proved Himself in the Bible many times, but He doesn't now. He seems kind of shy now. And inconsistent. 'Here's an absolute proof that you can check,' but there isn't one."

For Franky, old-timer atheist Bertrand Russell was a satisfying read. "He dismantles Pascal's wager," said Franky, "and I found his arguments for finding beauty and simplicity in living life without an afterlife to be very comforting. Still, Murray's book, *The Honest Atheist*, is the best one I have ever read. He freed me of all moral guilt."

"I know Horton Murray," I said.

"You know Horton Murray?" he asked, way too excited, like a contestant who has the chance of winning a new car. "Can you introduce me to him sometime?"

"Probably."

Franky is still young, I thought to myself. *Is he just going through his nihilism stage? Is this the latent teenage rebellion of a homeschooler who sees Christianity as rules to follow? Should his library card have been revoked? What moral standards was he using to judge the Bible?* There were a lot of questions I wanted to ask him at the time but didn't.

Just as we were about to end our conversation, Syd showed up with a fresh bottle of brew in her hands. *Was no one monitoring this person?*

"Let's go next door," she said to Franky. "They have whiskey."

"Well, Franky, thanks for explaining things to me," I said, standing up, trying to exit gracefully.

"What'd he explain?" Then she slurred something, which sounded like more profanity.

"He knows Horton Murray," Franky said.

She gave me a double take; but in her state, she really had no other option. At her alcohol level, everything was a double take.

"Did he tell you," she asked between hiccups, "educated people aren't religious? It's only the poor and ignorant."

"He did not happen to share that," I said. "But with all due respect, atheism is not an intellectual belief. It's an issue of the heart as demonstrated by the arrogance of your statement."

When I saw her fist coming, I only leaned back; and she missed me completely, swinging around fully, spinning herself into the ground. Even Franky couldn't help laughing at her buffoonish pratfall like she was reenacting some famous slapstick routine.

"And for my next trick . . ."

Franky took her by one arm. I tried to take her by the other to help her up, but she swatted at me and cussed. Franky and I looked at each other. His eyes told me it was okay to leave. At least, we ended our conversation without any arguments.

Franky and I liked each other. We liked the same things—movies, books, and good discussions. It was civil discourse. We had a lot in common, including a faith he once held. Though, we did have different tastes in women.

CHAPTER 9

"My nephew wants to meet you," I told Horton the next week at Starbucks.

"Can you trust me in person with him? I mean, look what my book did," he said as he neatly arranged his bagel on a napkin to prep it for cream cheese. You can make the correct assumption he ate it throughout our conversation as he sipped his grande iced chai, but I will spare you the details of his every bite and corresponding slurp.

"Oh, no," I said. "I figure once he meets you, he'll run back to Jesus."

"Like most of my dates."

"You had a date?"

"What are you? A comedian?"

"Isn't everyone?"

"It wasn't personal," he said. "What was the crux of his issue?"

"'Why no signs from God?'"

"Yeah," he said. "Sometimes we'll begin our meetings by inviting God to make the podium levitate. It's meant to be facetious."

"The assumption being a floating podium or a prophecy about God's signature under Forty-second and Broadway would be the miraculous key to believing. That's what my nephew requested."

"Interesting," he said. "But I do have to ask, if God exists, why doesn't He give your nephew what he's asking for?"

"Even your friends wouldn't believe if they saw a podium float."

"They wouldn't?"

"No. The Bible doesn't teach that if you see a miracle, you'll believe. Jesus performed His miracles in broad daylight. Lots of people saw Him and didn't believe. Seeing is not believing. That's a myth. Believing is seeing."[3]

"Wow, you should become a preacher," he said.

"Tim Allen said that in *The Santa Clause*."

He smiled, and I added, "The state of preaching today."

"You quote movies?"

"No," I said. "Just Tim Allen."

He laughed, then asked, "So, why wouldn't we believe if we saw a miracle?"

"Well," I said, "you and your friends of the floating podium society are basically saying, 'We don't believe there is a God. But if there is a God, then this is how He should act. But since He doesn't act that way, we don't believe in Him.'"

"I think I could win a debate with that premise."

"Really?"

"Next opportunity, I'm going to use that."

"Will you credit me?"

"Is it original with you?"

"None of my thinking is original."

"Then I'll take credit for it."

---

3   *The Santa Clause*, directed by John Pasquin, (1994; Burbank, CA: Walt Disney Pictures).

"No, you won't."

"Why not?"

"You're an honest atheist."

"Right," he said.

"Sorry to remind you."

"So, miracles aren't the key. Are they cheating, then?"

"Cheating?" I questioned.

"You know, you're supposed to have faith."

"I hope you're not giving me the 'faith is a blind leap into the dark' thing."

"Isn't it?"

"A blind leap in the dark is a leap into ignorance."

"I agree. But so far, the evidence is still unconvincing to me."

"That doesn't mean it's not good," I said, "just because you're personally unconvinced."

Horton and I covered this ground many times in our conversations, and I don't remember exactly what evidences we discussed in this instance. But here's a grainy highlight reel from our discussions:

According to Jesus, the Old Testament prophecies that were fulfilled in Him *are* God's signature under Forty-second Street in New York City. The very thing Franky was asking God to do, He did—and then some. The exact place of His birth was foretold and fulfilled. Riding into Jerusalem on a donkey was foretold and fulfilled. His betrayal was foretold and fulfilled. Gambling for His garments was foretold and fulfilled. The manner of His death was foretold and fulfilled. His resurrection was foretold and fulfilled, along with scores of other Old Testament prophecies that factually date long before He was even born. Isaiah 53 is the super-spreader of faith. It was written seven hundred years before the birth of Christ and five hundred years before the invention of crucifixion; yet it unmistakably describes the life, death, and resurrection of Jesus.

Plus, there were numerous witnesses to the resurrection. We have their testimonies recorded in the Gospels. Christianity has more extant documents than any other ancient literature. We have the explosive growth of the early church. We have the continued testimony of people today who claim to have met the risen Christ. Christianity is history, and it has shaped history like no other religion.

Deep breath. End of rant.

"Jesus rising from the dead is a historical claim, not a religious one," I said to Horton.

"It might be the religious version of historical events; I'll give you that."

"It has religious implications, sure; but first and foremost, it's a historical claim. There is complete historical consensus that Jesus lived and died and then went missing. Something happened to the body."

Theological somnambulation often overtook me in these conversations, as my unconscious spilled historical facts culled from Pop's lectures, books, and table-talk conversations between him and dinner guests, where eavesdropping as a child, I learned words like somnambulation.

The New Testament itself is the best evidence of the resurrection. As Pop always said, "Historians would fall all over themselves if they had this kind of record of the Peloponnesian War. Now, pass the ketchup."

Some of the best evidence (other than the New Testament documents themselves) comes from extra-biblical sources. The Talmud tells us Jesus went with His family to Egypt, returned to Judea with disciples and performed miracles with sorcery, led Israel astray, and was deserted at His trial without any defenders. In trying to discredit Jesus, they ended up verifying the Gospel accounts.

Suetonius (30-75 A.D.), the Roman historian, writes, "Why were Jews expelled from Rome in 48 A.D.? Because of a controversy over a certain Christ."

Tacitus referred to the crucifixion of Jesus under Pontius Pilate. Pontius Pilate has become one of the most famous historical figures ever because he is mentioned every Sunday in churches around the world reciting this little thing called The Apostles' Creed, which contains the phrase "suffered under Pontius Pilate."

Christianity is not a privatized faith but a public proclamation of the historical work of Jesus Christ. The most important evidence we have, therefore, is the resurrection itself, which is the point Jesus made in the parable of the rich man and Lazarus when He said, *"'If they do not hear Moses and the Prophets, neither will they be convinced if someone should rise from the dead.'"*[4]

These evidences all serve as God's signature to humanity. To Franky, they do not. To Horton, they're not convincing enough. And here we are.

"I like that your reasons at least sound reasonable," said Horton. "You're my favorite believer, you know."

---

4   Luke 16:31

"Oh, don't go too easy on me. I'll still be labeled as a fanatic."

"By my fellow atheists, I assume," he said.

"Only the bestselling ones."

"Well, of course. The ones who matter," he said with a grin. "Don't be discouraged. No matter how many books they sell, their code of ethics amounts to 'don't eat trans fats.' However rightly ridiculous they make faith out to be, their replacement ethic is just as ridiculous, if not more so."

"You said something like that to Bill Maher."

"I did."

"When the talk show hosts love you," I said, "it's a sign your philosophy isn't daring enough."

"Bill Maher liked me."

"Yes, and what does that say about you?"

"Libertarians are buying my book," he said.

"It is provocative."

His eyes grew wide with delight when I said this.

"Yes, I read your book," I said.

"Well, it was a free copy."

CHAPTER 10

It was one of those days when I wrote in spurts and fits, mostly just futzing around. Slumped in front of my faux-walnut desk, I piddled with emails, which led me to articles about this and that, sometimes related to a subject I was writing about so I counted those moments as research. But more often than not, I'd wander to the kitchen cabinet and snag five red licorice medallions. Why five? Because five equaled one hundred calories, which is what I counted, having given up on Atkins and everything else. Sitting at my desk chewing a licorice goody in the middle of piddling, Franky called.

"It's my nephew," I answered.

"I need your help," he said, sounding more serious than usual, which didn't take much.

"What is it?"

"Syd's been killed."

"What?"

"My date from the wedding."

"No," I said, "I remember who Syd is. How was she killed?"

There was a long silence, then, "She was murdered."

"Oh, Franky. I'm so sorry."

"We'd already broken up, but her father won't identify her body. He just keeps saying, 'No, no, no, that's not my daughter.' And her mother is presently unreachable, whatever that means. The point is, they've asked me to identify her body. And I'd rather not go alone."

"Sure, sure, sure. Absolutely," I said.

I met him at the County of Los Angeles Medical Examiner's building, which looked like it belonged in a 1940s crime drama. It was a handsome, old, red brick building with a white stone entry. Franky and I took the elevator to the lower level. The doors dinged, opened, and spat us into a hallway lined with linoleum, too light and bright for the occasion. The ventilation was different on this level—thick and scratchy to the nostrils, like remnants of aerosol cleaners hung in the air. The level was quiet, mostly empty; some orderlies (or attendants or whatever they happened to be) shuffled from room to room. It was like a hospital with no pressure.

We found the assigned room and were greeted by a tall and completely bald medical examiner with a slight forward hunch. He looked like the NBA version of Uncle Fester from the black-and-white *Adam's Family* television series. Had the situation not been so tragic, I might have laughed . . . or coughed to cover a laugh.

Uncle Fester looked at a clipboard and said, "Sydney Hawkins?"

Franky nodded.

"This way please," said Uncle Fester, leading us to a room next door. "I'm Dr. Harold Halula, by the way." I stand corrected. It wasn't Uncle Fester after all.

"We normally show you a photograph," said Harold, "but she's in really good condition, other than . . . well, yes . . . you understand. Anyway, you shouldn't be appalled or shocked by what you're about to see. She'll basically look like she's sleeping."

Then Dr. Halula (I still prefer Uncle Fester as a moniker) walked to the File Cabinets of Death and pulled on a handle. The squeak was unexpected, almost a clawing sound, very unsettling.

Once the file was halfway out, the doctor gently pulled back the sheet to reveal her head, and he was right—she appeared to be sleeping. With a hole in the side of her head. That much was clear—she had been shot in the head. Harold Halula had forgot to mention that.

Franky nodded to indicate it was her.

"Forgive me for asking," I said to Dr. Halula, "but is this type of murder unusual for rape victims? A shot in the head?"

"It is unusual, actually," he said. "Most are more violent—stabbing, choking, often with some object owned by the victim—but this . . . this was more execution-style. Like he didn't want to mess up her face."

"Interesting," I said, while feeling guilty for having the thought: *Could Franky have done this?* I scolded myself—*bad uncle*—for even wondering if he was capable of such a thing, but there it was shoving its way from the back of my mind to an actual conscious thought. Once the thought was there, it took over. *I think he did it.* Then I would correct myself. *You have no proof. You can't condemn people based on a hunch.* But the thought became even more adamant. *He did it. I know he did it.*

"She doesn't look bad for being dead," Franky said so casually that Dr. Halula's eyes narrowed for a moment.

Then it seemed he attributed Franky's socially insensitive statement to grief. "We do have a grief counselor on the premises who is available for family and friends of the deceased. We also have a room where you can take as much time as you need to process what you've just seen."

"Yup, yeah," said Franky. "Thanks, but we're good."

The detective in charge of the case wouldn't share any of the details of Syd's murder with Franky, other than the fact that her body was found in the Los Padres National Forest. Curious to know more, I called the one LAPD officer I knew, Officer Mike Shaw, an acquaintance who gave me his card once after a show and said if I ever got pulled over to show his card—something I would have never had the guts to do, but I kept his card in my wallet, anyway. Lo and behold, one night I was pulled over. While rummaging through my wallet to find my ID, I unknowingly flashed Officer Shaw's card; and the cop let me go. I didn't understand why he suddenly just told me to watch my speed and be on my way, until I thought about it afterward and realized he was shining his flashlight on my wallet while I shuffled credit cards and whatnot to get to my license. Anyway, Officer Shaw was kind enough to give me the lowdown on Syd's case.

It appeared she had run out of gas along a stretch of the road less traveled—Maricopa Highway, also known as Route 33. She was dating some shady new guy who lived out there, but someone else had picked her up. The shady guy had a solid alibi—he was making meth at the time. There were no witnesses or working cameras in the area; but whoever picked her up took her to a wooded area of the Los Padres National Forest, where she was shot in the head and then violated. As disturbing as that is, the most heartless act was whoever did this had staged her. They propped her up against a tree and placed a sign on her lap, block lettering from a home printer that said: *The Grand Experiment.*

My mind filled with accusatory thoughts again.

"Did they question you?" I asked Franky.

"Yup, yeah. I showed them our text exchanges that I had broken up with her and was concerned not only with her drinking but also that she had become addicted to the pain medication her doctor had prescribed. We had a big verbal blowout over it, and that was that; but it was kind of recapped through our text messages."

"The Grand Experiment," I said. "I wonder what that's all about."

"Who knows?" he said. "Probably drugs, if I know Syd."

The way he said it was so unsympathetic. I mean, we had just viewed her corpse; and I don't care what you think of a person, when you hear about the death of someone you know, however slightly, it's always accompanied by this sense of sadness. At least, it should be. Franky didn't seem sad. That's what bothered me. I hardly knew Syd Hawkins, but I was more troubled by her murder than Franky.

In a sentimental fit, I gave myself one last rebuke: *Franky has an odd personality, but that doesn't mean he's a psycho. Judging him like that is unfair. Suspicions are not an indication of guilt.*

Still, I decided I'd keep an eye on him.

CHAPTER 11

When my best comedy buddy, best man at my wedding, and best all-around L.A. friend, Evan, found out I was going to visit a monthly meeting of atheists led by Horton Murray, he invited himself along. And since I'd said I'd try to introduce him to Horton, I had already invited Franky.

My buddy Evan was a confirmed atheist when I first met him, but he now refers to himself as an agnostic Christian, meaning he doesn't get as mad during our discussions anymore. He's somewhat convinced but not enough to call himself a Christian. Evan has been very open about his problems with the Christian God; he sent me an email of several hundred words with twelve questions he wanted me to answer, which I did. They weren't easy questions— Old Testament genocide, rational grounds for the supernatural, why the repressive sexual ethic, etc. I sent Evan several thousand words back, answering his questions and concerns as best I could. He gave me books to read—Bart Ehrman's greatest hits, like *God's Problem*. I gave him *Ladies and Gentlemen, God: An Introduction* by Dr. Marcus Seitz, my own personal Pop, which Evan read and highlighted. We went to Panera Bread with Pop and discussed life and spirituality and how much better their bagels are than Starbucks' but how much better the drinks are at Starbucks. Why can't we all just get along?

Horton invited me to what he called "Atheists Anonymous." As it turned out, no one else there called it that. They called themselves the "Inland Empire Atheists." I told Horton they should just call themselves "Atheists Anonymous"—then they could franchise it. Everyone in the car that night agreed that "Atheists Anonymous" was a better name than "Inland Empire Atheists." It's more promising for slogans. *Atheists Anonymous: We don't believe in telling people we don't believe.* Or *Atheists Anonymous: Keep your unbelief to yourself.*

The Inland Empire Atheists and Agnostics, the official name on printed materials, used to be called the Inland Empire Freethinker's Club, but no one came. Probably because "Freethinkers" sounds like a group of wife-swappers left over from the sixties.

The Inland Empire Atheists, Agnostics, and Freethinkers meet at a church, which would be funny were it not a Unitarian church. Unitarianism is basically atheism with stained glass. Horton mentioned to the group they might be moving to a Mexican restaurant because some in the group found the stained-glass disconcerting. This wasn't even traditional stained glass with scenes of Jesus, Mary, and Joseph with angels above or halos over their heads or a dove surrounded by a starburst or anything. It was basically just decorative glass. Some people have such an aversion to church, they develop an emotional reaction to colored windows.

I know how they feel, in a way. I'm so opposed to atheism that I freak out whenever I open an empty suitcase.

Still, you are more apt to find strains of the historic Christian faith at the average Mexican restaurant than you are at the average Unitarian church. If God makes you nervous, then a Unitarian church is the best place for you because you won't find Him there. It seemed like the perfect place for a meeting of atheists to me.

I introduced Evan and Franky to Horton in the parking lot. Evan shook hands with him and said, "Pleasure to meet you." Standard. Normal. Franky shook hands with Horton and said, "If I ever have a child, I'm leaving it at your doorstep."

We all just nodded and grunted like, *Yeah, that's something someone just said,* to cover the bizarreness of his remark.

Upon entering the building, Horton, Evan, Franky, and I shook hands with a couple of young disbelievers; and Horton said, "Sam is a Christian comedian."

One of the young guys said, "That's great because we think Christianity's funny, too."

We each took a brown magic marker and wrote our names on the address labels provided and stuck them to our shirts. Directly behind me, I noticed an older, gray-haired gentleman, whose suit made him stand out from most of the crowd. There were three young men at the meeting who had earlobes stretched wide enough to knock a croquet ball through, so they stood out a little, too. Horton made a beeline for the older man and introduced me.

"Sam, this is Ron Derek. He's the speaker tonight."

Ron had been a teacher for thirty-three years and was now a school board member running for Congress in California's

Forty-fourth Congressional District, the District that panders to atheists. His topic was the separation of church and state.

"Are you an atheist yourself?" I asked.

"Oh, no. I'm . . . well, I'm of the Evangelical Lutheran persuasion but started out as a Presbyterian. But you know, Presbyterians don't last long. They study themselves right out of the faith. My four children are atheists."

Congratulations.

Before we took our seats, I glanced at a table full of atheist t-shirts. "Look at this," I said to Horton. "Even atheists have their kitsch."

There were three black shirts with white print to choose from, each with different sayings. One said, "Friendly neighborhood atheist." Then there was, "Teach science, not superstition." And finally, "Good without gods."

Even beyond the tacky t-shirts, there was an evangelical flair to the entire evening.

I leaned over to Horton and quietly said, "You're like a pastor."

That's when I first observed Franky wouldn't take his eyes off Horton. It wasn't a creepy stare but more a studied observation, though relentless. Horton was too busy to notice.

Horton went to the podium, still disappointingly flat on the ground, and introduced Ron, assuring everyone he wouldn't be partisan, as if the room wasn't full of left-leaning atheists who fawned over Marx. One of the jokes from my beginning days of standup was, "I used to be one of those people who doesn't believe in God. Whaddaya call 'em . . . uh . . . Democrats." It actually used to get a good laugh, but I have since opted for bipartisan comedy.

Ron was comfortable and winsome, projecting with his teacher's voice and forgoing the fuzzy-sounding microphone. The first subject he covered was standardized testing, which he was against. The stupidity of standardized testing is the test doesn't count toward the student's grade. Where's the motivation to not just fill in the circles with the number two pencil and get it over with? What a naive view of human nature and of teenagers in general. We were in complete agreement on this issue.

Then he transitioned to his grave concern over biology teachers who strayed from the state curriculum. He asked the group, "How do we reign in these teachers without seeming like insecure, little 'thought police'?"

Yeah, that's a tough one to pull off, I thought to myself.

He gave us an alarming statistic. "Sixteen percent of California biology teachers don't believe in evolution." Gasp. If your mouth hasn't fallen open yet, wait until you hear what he added. "And 9 percent refused to answer the question." That's more than 25 percent of California biology teachers who might possibly cause a ruckus.

"Science is based on fact." Ron said this more than once.

"Science is based on fact." That's twice now.

Let's hope scientific facts don't change as often as they have in the past because students in California have to use the same textbooks for seven years on average.

Ron pandered to the average atheist's overconfidence that science will eventually answer everything. That's a tall proposition, full of faith. Welcome to scientism, where science is left behind in the wake of assumptions. Where's the intellectual humility in that?

One of the main points of Horton's argument to his fellow atheists was that intellectual honesty requires deep skepticism when it comes to the naturalist worldview. Naturalism is orthodoxy (in the most religious sense possible) within the scientific establishment. And "any honest questioning leads to protests on the level of a rabid fundamentalist" was how Horton put it in his book.

The rabid fundamentalist vibe was all too apparent at the meeting that night, exemplified by their great concern over how to stop 16 to 25 percent of biology teachers from possibly saying anything negative about evolution. These concerned citizens were very concerned with preventing the spread of dissenting thoughts.

There was a polite applause break, and then Ron asked if there were any questions. Everyone subtly looked around to see who would go first, and I noted again Franky's gaze fixed upon Horton. At the time, I just thought to myself, *"This kid is a true fan,"* and wrote it off as nothing more.

That was before I noticed his gun.

CHAPTER 12

One of the young guys with hoop ears began the Q&A session by saying, "I'm going to play the devil's advocate here . . . "—which seemed an inappropriate thing for an atheist to say. I mean, if you don't believe in God, don't give the devil any credit either. Let's not play favorites here. Anyway, the devil's advocate brought up the idea that suppressing speech might be a bad thing. (Comedy at its best is just reporting because you can't make up stuff like this.)

The entire Q&A was fear-based. It was almost like being in a group of evangelical Christians. Maybe that's our common ground—being afraid of each other. Christians fear public schools are indoctrinating children with atheistic evolution, and atheists are afraid public discourse in science class will undermine evolutionary theory. It was almost as if we were all humans who shared a common ancestry.

On the plus side, when the Q&A ended, there was atheistic cheesecake and atheistic German chocolate cake and atheistic cookies and sodas, which all tasted very similar to Christian cheesecake and Christian German chocolate cake and Christian cookies and sodas. More common ground—we all use the same baker.

Cheesecake in hand, I mingled with some friendly neighborhood atheists. There was Miriam Olansky—who, with her maximum lips and a nose etched by some master, was easily the best-looking agnostic in the room. Suddenly, Horton had some competition. Franky had found a new and more attractive fixation. Miriam was not opposed to being called an atheist, I found out, and said she had converted to Mormonism at age sixteen.

"What was his name?" I asked.

She smiled at my question and then admitted there was a boy involved. This was back when she was in high school, which allowed her to mention she was valedictorian of her class. Then she used some words I didn't know, which confirmed that I was *not* valedictorian of my class. She left the fold of Mormonism (and all religion) at twenty after reading the King James Bible.

"They tell you to read the book, so I did," she said. "And that's why I left. I was too smart for the faith."

She was too smart for the Bible, yet I was pretty sure she didn't know how consciousness could be explained in the self-contained system of materialism. Never mind. One day, science will tell us. Just have faith.

I let it go. It was my impression she didn't read the Bible to find God; she only read the Bible, so she could say she read the Bible and it did nothing for her. Let it be noted, people can read the Bible with the wrong motives; and in that sense, you get out of it what you put into it. "You will seek me and find me, when you seek me with all your heart."[5] That Bible quote alone tells us motives matter when reading the Bible.

---

5   Jeremiah 29:13

There was another older lady who heard the "M" word, as she called it, and joined in our conversation with Miriam. She, too, was a former Mormon, raised in that religion with a Mormon mother who married a non-Mormon man, who she then divorced. This poor kid was doomed from the start. The Mormon community shunned her; so naturally, she became an atheist.

They both spoke of Mormonism as if it were a Christian denomination like Southern Baptist or Lutheran or Presbyterian or Methodist. I let that go, too; but just for your information, Mormonism is a new religion that's definitely not Christianity, though it reworked various aspects of the Christian faith. They use many of the same words but have completely different definitions for Jesus, God, and salvation than historic Christianity does. This is not to say Mormons aren't great neighbors and fine citizens. I'm just pointing out the fact Mormonism is a distinct religion from Christianity itself.

The last person who drifted into our circle was named Aaron. Miriam? And now Aaron? *Where's Moses? Let my people go!* I kept it all inside.

Actually, I already knew Aaron Belle but had never met his wife, Dawn, who was there also. Aaron is an on-again-off-again *Rolling Stone* journalist—on-again when he is sober and off-again when he is drinking—who also knew Horton because Horton's interview with Penn & Teller was published in an issue of *Rolling Stone*. Aaron had written a scathing critique of Contemporary Christian Music (is there any other kind?), for which he interviewed me (per Horton's recommendation) because I participated in some Christian music festivals as a comedian and emcee, where I mingled with all the bands who were being played on Christian radio with a mind-numbing frequency.

Aaron had a really long white beard tied off at intervals like a string of sausages. And that description doesn't do it justice. It was a really cool-looking beard that probably has a better name than "sausage beard." While writing periodically for *Rolling Stone*, Aaron was also working on his master's in journalism.

"What's your thesis on?" I asked, looking over to see if Miriam caught my astute usage of a word like "thesis."

His answer had something to do with internet-based local news sources. Back then, there were only a few in the country that covered a local area and didn't have a print edition.

"Good luck with that," said Evan.

"*Rolling Stone* will probably abandon the print magazine in the next few years," he said.

"You think so?" I asked, being one who was still enamored with print.

"It's the wave. Gotta catch the wave."

His wife, Dawn, was studying spatial measurements having to do with maps—not only maps but primarily maps.

"My favorite maps are the ones where the mountains are little bumps," I told her. "Make more of those."

Aaron wore those shoes that are shaped exactly like feet with a separate area for each toe and rubber bottoms that followed the contours of his soles—those shoes that make you look like you are barefoot with a fungus. But in a cool way.

Horton always ribbed Aaron about his white beard because he looked like Santa Claus doing a commercial for Jenny Craig.

He had rosy cheeks and a white beard but not enough jolly in his belly to get hired by Gimbels. (Since they were atheists, I figured a department store that doesn't exist was more appropriate.) Horton called Aaron an "uncommitted atheist"—what others would call an "apatheist," meaning he just doesn't care to believe. Aaron called himself a leaky atheist.

Initially, Franky was so starstruck with Horton he couldn't think of anything to say. But wanting to impress him, he started telling a story of his latest political protest against some new California measure being proposed. Miriam said she had been part of a corner protest once with her eight-year-old daughter when a family drove by in an SUV and tossed a plastic cup full of Coke that hit her little girl.

"That was very Christian of them," she said.

I'm not sure why she assumed they were Christians; but if Christianity is false, then is it really fair to hold people accountable to their own imaginary standards?

I held it inside, looked at my empty paper plate, then looked back at the group.

"I'm still hungry," I said. "Anyone else?"

CHAPTER 13

After exhausting our resources inside the Unitarian church (the atheistic cheesecake no longer existed), Horton, Aaron (his wife had to leave), Evan, Franky, Miriam, and I walked next door to Mario's, an upscale restaurant, where a lively and friendly discussion ensued. These folks didn't have to wear t-shirts that said, "Friendly neighborhood atheist." They lived it.

"I don't really like calling myself an atheist," said Franky. "I don't want to be defined by what I don't believe. I view myself more as a philosopher if one must label me."

"You might wanna take off your name tag," I said.

He ignored me and went on. "The question, 'Does God exist?' is no more relevant than the question, 'Does a fuzzy pink bunny exist?' Because neither one is verifiable. I can say, 'God created this glass,' or I can say, 'A fuzzy pink bunny created this glass.' Yes, you see, they are both meaningless statements."

"Unless you die and find yourself standing before a fuzzy pink bunny," I said.

"Then you better hope he's really fuzzy," said Evan.

"But the question of God's existence is a valid question," I said to my nephew, who was exhausting the collected vocabulary of his short twenty-one-year-old life span to impress Horton. "If it was meaningless, you wouldn't be gathering with a group of other like-minded people who question belief in God. The gathering we just came from proves the validity of the question. There is a reason people don't gather together to affirm their disbelief in the Easter Bunny. It's not in the same category."

"Even if you rename God as 'a fuzzy pink bunny' or 'the flying spaghetti monster,' we still know Who you're really talking about," said Evan, and I was happy he was on my side because he usually wasn't.

Franky said, "Yup, yeah. Sure. Believing in Jesus is about as *rational* as believing in Santa Claus or the Tooth Fairy."

"Really?" I said. "Franky, that is such a profoundly ignorant statement."

"You're just biased because of family ties," he said.

"Just because I'm biased doesn't mean it can't be true."

"We've given Jesus too much credit . . . too, too much," said Franky.

I nearly lost it. "You're just . . . I can't even . . . " But then I recovered. "It's simply a fact. Jesus Christ changed the world. No one will ever say that about Santa Claus or the Tooth Fairy. They are simply not in the same category as an infinite, personal, Creator God, Who has no beginning and no end."

"Yeah," said Evan. "No one is writing books about Santa Claus not being great."

"It can be safely said that Santa Claus has *disappointed* everyone who has ever believed in him," I said.

Miriam and Aaron both laughed at that one, but I was being serious.

"Comparing belief in Jesus with belief in Santa Claus is simply a ridiculous argument, and people should stop using it," I said.

Then Franky adjusted himself in his seat, and I saw he had a concealed handgun in a shoulder holster under his windbreaker. I scanned the group to see if anyone else spotted it. No such luck.

Okay, don't freak out, I told myself. *He could have a permit. Concealed carry is perfectly legal. You're not a gun owner, so don't jump to conclusions just because you think he already murdered someone. Calm down.*

"Speaking of Santa Claus," said Horton, "nothing personal, Aaron, but roping off your beard ain't foolin' no one."

"It keeps the children away," said Aaron.

"And the waitstaff, apparently," said Evan, scouting the place for service. When he finally caught someone's attention, we ordered drinks.

Undeterred after nearly downing his beverage, Franky plunged forward with his testimony of defection. "I'm just thankful science corroded away my religious belief, you see," he said.

"Thankful to whom?" I asked, though a little less forcefully now that I knew he was packing heat. "You can't even account for why we're aware of ourselves."

"You need to clarify that," said Horton.

"Really? I got it from you."

"Did I say it like that?"

"No, you said it like a smart person," I said. "But the gist was that, somehow, matter became conscious of itself and began to examine itself. You said that demands an explanation."

"I'll give you that," Horton said. "We have no answer for consciousness. No good answer, anyway. But we're still evolving."

"Then how can we even trust our own observations of ourselves if we're not fully evolved yet?" I asked.

"That *is* kind of self-undermining, isn't it?" said Horton

"You *are* an honest atheist," Evan said.

"These are issues naturalism cannot account for," Horton said. "I've admitted that."

"And yet believing God created all things is unreasonable somehow," I said.

Our server finally appeared again, and Evan asked what menu items might be ordered this late. He was told only appetizers.

Maybe Aaron felt it was a great injustice they closed off portions of their menu to us late-nighters, or maybe it was because Horton had conceded a couple of points; but Aaron suddenly looked at me and asked, "How do you explain a God who would kill babies?"

He sounded a little testy, which was unusual for Aaron, but he had drunk two beers.

I had two Cokes, so I was only jittery.

"That's the question," I said. "Why is drowning babies wrong?"

"Why is it wrong?" gasped Miriam.

"Hey, you don't know these babies," I said. "They could be baby Hitlers."

That was followed by some laughter, some gasps.

"So, you *are* against drowning babies," said Aaron. "Unlike your God."

"Okay, lemme ask you this," I said to the group. "If you could go back in time and eliminate baby Hitler, would it be morally right to do so?"

"Assuming you knew you could prevent the deaths of the sixty million people who died because of the war he started," added Evan.

"Yes," I said. "Would you do it? Also, you've been given limited foreknowledge and a limited gift for time travel."

"A limited gift?" asked Evan.

"Okay, here's the second part of the hypothetical killing baby Hitler scenario," I said. "You are allowed to go back in time and do away with baby Hitler, but no one will know you've been given a time-traveling pass. You will just go down in history as a baby-killer. Would you still do it?"

"Assuming we get caught," said Aaron, "can't I kill baby Hitler and travel back to the future with no one the wiser?"

"No. You can only travel back in time, but then you have to stay and face the consequences," I said.

"The logical problem with time travel is that someone from the present cannot go back and change the past," said Horton. "Think about it. If you effected change in the past, your future self would have already experienced said change and there would be no reason for you to time travel to the past."

"What?" asked Evan.

"If you go back and successfully kill baby Hitler, then in the present—because you've been successful in the past—you would have no reason to travel back in time and kill baby Hitler because he'd already be dead," said Horton. "It's paradoxical."

"Holy moly, never engage with a professional," I said.

Most everyone laughed, but I could tell Franky had been sitting there stewing about something. Of course, none of us realized the conversation to follow would change the course of our lives by involving everyone in a murder investigation.

CHAPTER 14

Things quieted down, and Franky asked the group, "Why do we even want to save these sixty million people?"

We all looked at Franky, then at each other.

"Because they're human beings," said Miriam, speaking for the group.

"Ah, you're covertly religious," Horton said to her.

"I am not."

"If you're trying to smuggle in the inherent value of human beings, you are because you can't claim such a thing without a Deity."

"Science can prove murder is a universal evil," she said.

"Really?" asked Horton. "How does science do that?"

"Neuroscience," said Miriam. "The well-being of human beings can be measured by brain activity. We all respond the same to pleasure and pain. It's measurable."

"I find atheists who argue for a universal morality based upon neuroscience to be as frightening as the religious demagogues they fear," said Horton, "because they are both arguing for an absolute morality based upon revelation. It's just that one revelation comes from science and the other from a god. They're still both revelations that fool people into speaking in terms of moral absolutes they feel everyone should follow. That's the kind of thinking that will lead my fellow atheists into the religious wars they so self-righteously condemn."

"Stop doing bits," I said.

Evan and Aaron laughed.

"The problem is they're simply replacing one faulty foundation of morality for another," said Horton. "That's all they did in the French Revolution. They replaced Divine authority with human authority. That's why it became oppressive and violent—because the foundation was still absolutist."

"And your point is there isn't one," said Aaron. "There's no foundation."

"Exactly," said Horton. "There is no supreme source, no benchmark of absolute, eternal truths. But people don't like that because it makes social-political arguments harder to sell. You lose your moral indignation. And man, are my academic brethren ever selling a narrative of moral indignation these days. I fear the next generation."

"I'm surprised your book sold," I said.

"I'll be yesterday's news sooner than later. Believe me. There's a new wave of optimistic atheists on the horizon. In reaction to my work, I think."

"Optimistic atheism? How's that work?"

"Life has no meaning, but you can pretend it does."

"No? Really?"

"They dress it up more, but that's the idea when you strip it down."

"That's just plain dumb."

"There is no greater stupidity than a stupid intellectual," he said.

Now it was my turn to laugh, and I said, "Did you write that?"

"I think Benjamin Franklin said it," he said. "But I've never been able to verify the quote."

"Then it's yours. Can I use it? I think it makes a great title: *The Stupid Intellectual.*"

"Feel free—if you write my biography one day."

"Are you saying human flourishing isn't an undeniable good?" asked Miriam.

"What makes human flourishing an undeniable good?" Horton asked back. "The fact that you feel that way? You've made pleasure the highest moral absolute. There's no reason to do that. You've done so arbitrarily. It's utilitarianism with a brain scan. Not only that, it's hedonistic utilitarianism."

"What's utilitarianism?" asked Evan.

"Whatever makes the most people happy is considered a moral good," I said and looked at Horton.

"That's as good a definition as any of the stupid intellectuals give," he said.

"So, it's okay to drown babies," Miriam said to Horton.

"If there is no God," said Horton, "then there are no inherent rights for anyone—the fetus or the mother or anyone else. Universal morality simply doesn't exist."

"Unless God exists," I said.

"Of course."

"And if He doesn't?"

"That's the problem with Hume, Kant, and all the rest, including Rand," said Horton. "They tried to create grounds for morality apart from God. All I'm saying is it's a failed argument. We just have to admit there are none in a universe that is alone."

"'Everything is permissible,'" I said, quoting some Dostoevsky character.

"It's the logical premise of my atheism, and it's the only honest conclusion," he said.

"*The Honest Atheist.*"

"At your service," he said with a slight bow.

"I think he just said it's okay to drown babies," said Evan.

"He thinks it's okay to drown anyone," I said. "Don't you know you're talking to the man who made nihilism popular?"

"What's nihilism?" asked Evan.

"Please, try and keep up," I said in an artificial reprimand. "If we come from nothing, then nothing has meaning." And I looked at Horton again.

"You're right on par with stupid smart people," he said.

"I hope so," I said. "I was quoting you."

"It was a paraphrase," said Horton, while shaking his hand back and forth to indicate it was off a little. "You dumbed it down."

"To keep on par," I said.

"Here's the issue," said Horton. "Claiming any rights in an absolute way is affirming the existence of God. That's why I, as an atheist, can't do it. We can't claim something as an absolute inherent right. Either our standard for justice is outside of us, or it's arbitrary. If justice is arbitrary, which it must be in atheism, then a culture somewhere that decides drowning babies is a good idea can't really be condemned by us or anyone else."

"I can't believe you would drown a world of babies," said Miriam.

"Wait a second," I said. "You think it's okay to kill a world of babies as long as they're still in their mother's belly."

"It's not the same thing," she said.

"Oh, right—location, location, location," I said.

Horton intervened. "If there is no God, then everything is permitted—one of Ivan's theories in *The Brothers Karamazov*—but it is the right conclusion when we admit our premise."

"I don't believe in a god, and I'm a moral person," said Miriam.

"That's fine," said Horton. "All I'm saying is that it doesn't matter. Nothing matters is the point of a universe that comes from nothing."

"I don't believe that," said Miriam.

"Well, explain purpose to me in a purposeless universe," he said.

"I determine meaning and purpose for my life," she said. "I have a very fulfilling life. I enjoy my work. I find it meaningful. I love my daughter."

"Ah ha," he said to Miriam with an ironic wink, meaning an over-exaggerated one because a traditional wink might be misinterpreted. (It's probably best in today's cultural climate to stay away from winks altogether.) "You're an optimistic atheist. All well and good, but you must see that any meaning you give these things is illusory."

"It's real to me," she said.

"But it doesn't go beyond you," he said. "If there is no transcendent meaning, then all you can do is pretend there is meaning, which is nothing but self-deception. That's my argument against my fellow atheists today. We must accept the simple conclusion of our atheism—nothing matters. If there is no God, then morality is simply a human construct."

"But we've evolved into social beings," said Miriam. "We have feelings for other people. It's built into the fabric of who we are. It's what we have to do to get along with other creatures. It's programmed into human nature to want to get along. No one wants to live in a society where everyone is murdering and raping everyone else."

Then Franky laughed a little too hard.

There was an awkward pause, the only kind associated with Franky; and then we all looked at him and waited.

CHAPTER 15

Miriam's remark had been serious; but as was often the case in conversations with multiple personalities involved, sometimes something said was unintentionally funny. I didn't think this was one of those times, but I was interested in Franky's state of mind. I think his chilling cackle made everyone a little curious to see if he had a thought to go with it. My eyes were probably on him first, since I had kept him in my peripheral vision during most of the conversation for obvious reasons.

Once he wiped the drool of his laugh away, Franky said, "No one wants to live in a society where everyone is murdering and raping? Well, that depends on what neighborhood you grew up in. There are parts of San Bernardino County where murder *is* a way of life. Everyone is murdering everyone else; so apparently, that's how some people want to live."

"You've created a monster," I said to Horton, but he laughed it off.

"But my question is this," said Franky. "If everything is permitted, will a person who believes that be willing to do anything?"

"Yes and no," said Horton. "As Miriam has pointed out, societies have evolved; and the self-preservation instinct has produced laws to protect our survival."

"So, it's not wrong to murder, morally speaking, but getting caught is undesirable?" said Aaron.

"That's the idea," said Horton. "We prefer pleasure to pain. That's fine. But that doesn't give pleasure meaning. It doesn't make human flourishing an absolute moral good."

"Why not?" asked Miriam.

"Okay, I'm gonna go out on a limb here," Horton said. "When we die, we cease to exist. Nothingness. How does anything we do now ultimately matter? It simply doesn't. But for some reason, we can't seem to face that. One day, humanity itself will become extinct, and nothing we've ever done will matter in the least."

"Very few people are willing to go where the evidence leads," said Franky.

"So, nothing is wrong?" Miriam asked Horton.

"In an absolute sense? Nothing."

"So, you'd kill me?" she asked him.

"In self-defense? Sure."

"No. Murder," she said.

"I don't want to murder you," said Horton. "But if I had to murder you for some strange reason, dust to dust."

"Thanks for the sympathy," she said.

"Well, I'd rather not," said Horton, "because it would rob me of your presence, which I find very pleasant."

She blushed.

"An even better question," said Franky, wanting to destroy any spark between Horton and Miriam, "would you rape her? If you had the chance and knew you could get away with it?"

His question was followed by a few moments of silence, during which everyone but Franky cringed.

Miriam said to Horton, "Well, would you?"

"Rape isn't about sex," said Horton.

"C'mon," said Aaron. "Don't evade the question."

"Yeah," said Evan. "What happened to the honest atheist?"

"I don't want to embarrass her," said Horton.

"It sounds to me like you would rape me," said Miriam.

"Sure, I would," said Horton, "but then I'd have to kill you, too. So, it's just not practical."

Miriam laughed at this and said, "That's a yes!"

If the conversation wouldn't have been so oddly dark, I would have sworn Horton and Miriam were flirting with each other. Everything was said tongue-in-cheek, of course. It looks worse in print than it sounded during the banter because the tone was not threatening at all. Granted, it's not the kind of stuff you hear on your average family sitcom, but I could be wrong. I don't watch much T.V. anymore. Besides, I don't think the average family sitcom exists any longer.

"I can't believe you would rape and kill me," said Miriam gleefully, like it was a compliment somehow.

"You must not be familiar with his book," I said to her.

"No, I'm not. I've heard of it, of course." When she said this, she looked at Horton like she wanted to reassure him. "I'll have to get a copy."

"I have one in the car," said Horton. "I'll give it to you when we leave if you like."

"Yes, I'd like that," she said.

"After that conversation, I wouldn't walk anywhere with this guy after dark," said Evan.

"Oh, I think he's harmless," said Miriam.

"I wouldn't be too sure," said Franky but without a humorous tone.

"He's part of a debate next week if you'd like to join us," I said to Miriam.

"So, are you debating a Christian?" she asked Horton.

"Three Christians. It's a debate between three Christians and three atheists."

"Even better," she said.

"We'll get to the bottom of what they're teaching in biology class one way or another," said Evan.

We all laughed. Just like in a sitcom.

CHAPTER 16

The air was chilly—by California standards, anyway—as I sat outside our apartment waiting for Horton to arrive in his brand-new BMW 525. I've never been much for cars—shiny evidence of the upper hand—but Franky had repeated the make and model so often and with such admiration that I knew it by heart. Horton had invited me over for dinner. Maybe it was the intimacy of someone else's home, but I never could get him to set foot inside our apartment. Maybe it was the new baby. George didn't cry a lot; and by the time anyone came over, he was usually asleep. But maybe Horton was just uncomfortable with the idea of being around a baby.

My wife, Lana, and I had only one car at the time, and she took it with George to visit her mom in Thousand Oaks; so Horton picked me up and drove me to his place, which was splayed on a hill in Eagle Rock like a tribute to his celebrity status. Thanks to his book, Horton was probably worth about two million dollars at that point. He was working on a second book called *The Amoral Universe*.

"You should put a picture of your house on the cover," I told him. The advance for the new book alone was enough to pay for his "pad," which is what I always called it because he was a bachelor, after all, but also because the neighborhood where he lived had such a hipster feel. The house had been built on the top of a hill sometime in the seventies, and Horton had it renovated to look like a futuristic Jetsons' home with lots of glass and sleek cabinets and mod furniture. The only thing missing was a robot maid.

When I arrived, Horton introduced me to his sister, Pam, who was fluffing couch pillows, the closest thing to pets in their sanitized world. She was tall and slender, offering eye contact that made me feel dumb and exposed but not judged—perfect for an authentic relationship with some guy she hadn't attracted yet.

She owned a prop company in Los Angeles, which she had inherited from their father, who was also a prop master—a vocation he inherited from his father, which is still how people land jobs in show business. Horton had a photo hanging on a wall in his home of his grandfather holding a cub of the MGM lion like a little baby. Even lions got their gigs through nepotism. His grandpa had been the prop man for *The Wizard of Oz*.

There's a lot you can learn about a person by visiting their home, especially if they have stuff on the walls like diplomas and family photos and famous artwork of living people I had never heard of before.

Horton went to USC before he decided to venture east for his doctorate—not that he was a stranger to the East Coast. Another thing Horton and I had in common was that we both went to private boarding schools, though Horton went to the top boarding school in the country, Phillips Exeter Academy in New Hampshire. The boarding school I attended doesn't even rank in the top fifty in the nation. Exeter is always ranked number one or number two, and their style of teaching helped Horton become an excellent debater.

"It's a special occasion," Pam said, handing me a drink.

"What's the occasion?" I asked.

"You are the first human being, other than myself, to set foot in this house," she said.

"Don't be mean," I said. "Atheists are human, too."

Pam laughed at me, so I liked her immediately.

"Her statement is untrue, anyway," said Horton. "Just last week, there was a carpenter who finished my closet shelves."

"Oh, you should have invited him," said Pam. "I meet so few carpenters."

She sat on the couch and kicked her feet up with great exaggeration, placing them on the ottoman.

"You're married, I suppose," she said.

"Yes, I am," I answered like a schoolboy in trouble, back when children felt guilty in school for being in trouble.

"Oh, well, I know I'm nothing to look at," she said confidently.

"You don't try," said Horton.

"Oh, a little lipstick will do the trick, will it?" she said.

"You know what I mean, dear."

"Don't start with the *dear*," she quipped, turning to me. "That's his patronizing name for me."

"How close are you two in age?" I asked, just then realizing I may have broken a rule of social engagement about a woman's age but also thinking, *Who even knows what a social taboo is to men or women these days?*

"I'm the baby," said Pam. "And that's all you need to know."

"Of course," I said.

"So, who is this Miriam I've been hearing so much about?" she asked me.

"He talks about her?"

"He talks *to* her on the phone." Then she jerked out her arm and brought her hand back to her face in the shape of a phone, using her pinky and thumb to mimic each end, and imitated her brother. "Mmhmm, yes. I think so, too." All her gestures were purposely overdone like she was on stage.

"Those are private calls," he said.

"Not when I can hear them," she said, and I laughed.

"You laughed," she said to me. "I had assumed you wouldn't laugh at anything anyone said, being a comedian and all."

"Well, it is true. Comedians are not big laughers, but I have learned to express my appreciation for a joke because of that very fact. I make a horrible audience, and I don't want anyone to be a horrible audience."

"Here, here," she said and clapped.

"You two are like old school chums already," Horton said.

"Don't be jealous, dear," she said. "I won't steal your only friend."

"Don't you start with the *dear*," he said. "That's her patronizing name for me."

"You two are like brother and sister," I said.

"Is stating the obvious a type of humor?" said Pam.

"I guess not, since you didn't laugh."

Then something dinged in the kitchen, and Horton said, "Uh oh."

"What?" I asked.

"Dinner is served," he said.

CHAPTER 17

We all moved to the sleek white kitchen table which stood in front of a glass plate wall overlooking the lights of Los Angeles below, which were beautiful in a Tower of Babel kind of way—had the tower been horizontal. The meal was traditional lasagna with garlic bread, and that's it—oh, yeah, and a salad, but a salad to me is always like a less popular guest no one speaks to once the other guests arrive.

"So, Pam, where are you on the atheist-theist spectrum?" I asked.

"Oh, I don't give either two thoughts," she said.

"She hasn't even read my book," said Horton.

"I tried," she said. "It's just not a conversation that interests me." And then she mouthed, "Boring," while pointing to Horton like her hand was a blinking neon sign.

"It's not mystical enough for Pam," he said.

"I'm not mystical," she said. "I'm completely secular."

"You interpret dreams," he said.

"That's just a lark," she said.

"Tell her one of your dreams, Sam. She'll give you the lowdown."

"Oh, no, thank you," I said. "I've had quite enough of that."

"Of dreams?" she asked.

"It's a long story," I said.

"He wrote a book about it," said Horton.

"Now that might interest me," she said. "Horty dismisses me, even though I pegged one of his dreams. But he won't admit it."

"There's nothing scientific about it," he said.

"It's a soft science," said Pam.

"Quackery," said Horton.

Ignoring him, she looked around as if the room was full and she was deciding upon who to approach. "Hmm, she said. "What we need is a witness."

Horton rolled his eyes.

"Don't be a spoiled sport, *dear*," I said, and Pam laughed.

"I don't remember most of my dreams," he said.

"Just give me the last one you remember," said Pam.

He gave her a mothering expression, which told her to behave in front of the guest.

"Please," she said, drawing out the word.

"Whatever," he relented. "Okay, the other night I dreamed that Franky, Sam's nephew, was at the top of a cliff, and I'm at the bottom. I'm trying to persuade him not to jump, but he jumps anyway. But before he hits the ground . . . suddenly, it's me falling. Then I woke up."

All the blood in Pam's face dashed away, leaving her pale.

We both noticed it.

"What?" Horton said.

"What do you mean, 'what?'" she asked, striving to recover.

"You have an interpretation or not?" he said.

"Oh, what's the . . . It doesn't matter, anyway. You're right," she said. "It's not scientific." Then she stood up with her plate. "How about dessert?" But I could see her arm shaking.

"You're avoiding the question," he said. "Whatever you think it means, it would only affect me if I believed in dream interpretation, which I don't. So, just tell us. For the sake of curiosity."

"Mascarpone and dark chocolate cream in white chocolate cups," she said. "Direct from the local bakery."

"You're more like Mother than you'll admit," he said.

After dessert, Horton showed me a manuscript his mother wrote that was a kind of amalgam of pseudo-religious and scientific thoughts on life called *Then God Laughed: The Relativity of Science and the Bible for Young Adults.* And this was years before *Saturday Night Live* alum Julia Sweeney wrote her one-woman show *God Said, Ha!* So, his mother was a trailblazer in that sense. In her spiritual-seeking frenzy, she had even had Horton baptized at Faith Tabernacle in Los Angeles, though Horton, being only eight at the time, didn't understand what was happening. He remembers it— and not fondly. His mother, a seeker of gurus and crackpots—not that she would characterize them as such—treated spiritual fads like a jelly of the month club. Horton denied this had anything to do with him becoming an atheist, but he did admit this is why he developed his critical thinking skills because his mother never seemed to scrutinize anything deeply.

"Take a peek at it," he insisted, regarding the manuscript. "Anywhere will do. Linear thinking didn't matter in her world."

So, I randomly turned to a page and silently read to myself, *Of course, the Milky Way is only one of many galaxies (disks composed of billions of stars) which float in God's vast universe. Indeed, the Milky Way system, like other galaxies, probably contains a multitude of heavenly bodies with environments similar to earth. No doubt God has set up life on these other planets, too.*

In fact, the apostle John has told us, "In my Father's house are many mansions . . . "⁶ And as our spaceships penetrate even more deeply into outer space, we shall probably come to visit these other mansions—or civilizations, as we call them nowadays.

Never mind that the apostle John is referring to Heaven here and not *the* heavens, as in outer space. In any case, Horton honed his cerebral skills of reasoning thanks to his mother's *A Course in Miracles* confusion.

"She could probably get this thing published today," I said.

"Oh, yeah," said Horton. "She was ahead of the spiritistic curve. Like Pam here."

"It's not spiritual," said Pam. "It's psychological. The study of the mind."

"Anyway," said Horton, "it's something."

"I rather think it's just a lark," said Pam with hope in her voice, but I sensed it was a self-deceptive hope.

---

6   John 14:2 KJV

CHAPTER 18

Evan, my agnostic Christian buddy, picked me up on the way to the debate between the three atheists and three Christians, so we could listen to people from both sides of the issue talk over each other with the aid of microphones. We drove to Orange County, where we stopped at his friend Garry's house. Evan warned me several times that Garry is "a New York Jew who can be a little abrasive." Garry did not live up to the hype. He did have a slight New York accent, and he continually shot out one-liners like he was auditioning for a chance to play Henny Youngman on Broadway; but his demeanor was that of a sweet retiree who's been happily married for thirty-six years to the same woman.

During the intermission, right in the middle of our own debate within the debate, Garry interrupted us all and said, "Hold everything! I just saw a t-shirt that I love. It said, 'My Wife Rocks.'" End of announcement.

You can't help liking a man who loves his wife like that.

As soon as we set foot in Garry's house, he started giving Evan a hard time, but good-naturedly, in the way of old friends. They knew each other from AA. Garry had been Evan's sponsor, a task I would wish upon no one.

"You're only twenty minutes late," said Garry, "so you're actually early. Twenty minutes—that's nothin' for you."

"There was traffic."

"Something you weren't expecting? Get out more . . . of my house."

"Garry, this is Sam."

"You're, Sam? Sam I am?" Then he waved his arms around to introduce me to his home. "I started out with nothing and still have most of it left."

Evan looked at his watch and said, "We should probably get going."

"Hey, just use your shoes to walk anywhere around our house."

"You have shoes on," Evan said.

"They're indoor shoes. You have on outdoor shoes."

"Are we going?"

Garry had a new hybrid car with a trunk that only opened when it scanned his fingerprints. It also had a camera mounted somewhere in the trunk, so he could see the trashcans he backed over.

"Oops. Doesn't matter. They're plastic."

"This car is amazing," I said.

He said, "If you think nobody cares if you're alive, try missing a couple of car payments."

I swear I heard a snare drum in his trunk, too.

As mentioned, Garry is Jewish, attends temple, has two sons who were bar mitzvahed, and travels the world with his wife, whom he would like to proclaim his affection for on a t-shirt. They've been to thirty-five countries—all on the pension of a retired math teacher. (Can math teachers be on the take?)

"I pretended to work," said Garry. "They pretended to pay me."

Garry is not an atheist. He's just what you would call unenthusiastically religious. He believes—but not really, not too much.

"People take religion too seriously," was how Garry put it. "Evan, you should do some soul-searching. You just might find one."

Getting lost and then blaming Evan via a string of jokes, Garry finally found the street and picked up Franky, the newly elected president of Horton Murray's fan club. Franky and Evan have similar demeanors—dark and caustic—while Garry is high-strung in a fun way. I can hardly keep quiet during any debate. We were on our way, the Four Horsemen of the Apologists—an agnostic Christian, a Horton zealot, a nominal Jew, and me, a born-again comedian. Debate or bust.

Miriam met us there.

"We could've picked you up," Franky said to her, his voice tinged with concern over her travel arrangements.

"I appreciate that; but clearly, I made it," she said.

I could tell Miriam was trying to discourage him because she was a few years older than Franky but not quite young enough to be out of range on Horton's dating service profile, if he ever had one.

"Did you drive?" Franky asked, ignoring all the signals she was giving him about not pursuing this line of questioning.

"No," said Miriam, scanning the room to find us a place to sit but really only to avoid eye contact with Franky. "You guys wanna sit closer or further back?"

"How'd you get here?" asked Franky, as zealots tend to be persistent.

Realizing it would be found out sooner or later, Miriam resigned herself and said, "Horton picked me up."

"Oh," said Franky with a woebegone face. "You drove over with Horton?"

"Turns out we live near each other," she said as if proximity was the main reason.

"Hey, let's find some seats," I said, a statement of orange cones to move the focus another direction, away from Franky's pining for Miriam.

"Let's sit in the middle," said Garry. "That way, we can be more objective."

The debate was held at the Costa Mesa Community Center, which is a cold, concrete structure that beckons people to stay away—the perfect place for fostering community. Still, around one thousand people showed up; and when the moderator surveyed the crowd, it was split evenly between atheists, agnostics, and Christians. There were seven people who believed in unicorns, but all groups shunned them. This is one issue where atheists and Christians find common ground—those unicorn people are nuts. You probably think I'm being flippant, but I'm not.

There was a man sitting behind me who wore a t-shirt that read, "Unicorns are real." I pointed and asked him, "Really?" He spouted the website address, which contained the hard evidence, then offered, "Unicorns have always been evasive and difficult for science to study."

"Okay," was all I said because it can be dangerous to confront people's delusions.

Even more shocking, I found out the debate was a ticketed event—a fundraiser for the atheists' club. Didn't they know our money still said, "In God we trust"? This did not stop them from taking it and saying with a smirk, "We'll see about that." I didn't hear them say this aloud, but I'm sure they were thinking it. And they may not have actually smirked, but they looked like they were smirking, if you squinted your eyes at them. Thankfully, Evan had made reservations, which saved me five bucks, so I had a little trust left.

They blinked the lights, letting us know the debate was about to begin—something I suspected they stole from Penn & Teller.

CHAPTER 19

Horton's debate team had an interesting strategy that completely baffled the Christians. In his opening statement, Horton said, "The first thing we'd like to do is concede the God question for the sake of argument. However, if there is a God . . . "

Horton and his team of atheists weren't debating the laws of science or the existence of God. They were debating theology.

Horton continued his opening thought with the question, "Is it just for God to send people to Hell forever?"

Horton and his team repeatedly hammered this point; and by their answers, the Christian debaters demonstrated the unbelievable shallowness of some sectors of evangelicalism (sector nine to be exact—I'm not telling you where that is, but it's close to Atlanta.) When was the last time you even heard a sermon on God's wrath or Hell in an evangelical church? (The answer is *never* if you live in sector nine.)

As stated in the programs, the theme of the debate was "Does the God of the Bible Exist?" (And if He does, where can I apologize?) Horton's team targeted the God of the Bible.

"You see?" I whispered to Evan. "Deep down, there is only one God we fear—the Christian one. So, atheists can stop with the small-g God stuff. We all know Who they're talking about, and it's not Zeus."

Both Christians and atheists in the crowd found some common ground in the ineptitude of this panel of Christian apologists. That isn't to say they were unqualified, but their strategy made them ineffectual. They wouldn't engage the question at hand, whatever it happened to be, instead sticking to their talking points about the existence of God, the very point the atheists had conceded from the get-go. And the one Christian debater's plugs for his products became so overbearing that at one point, the 50 percent of atheists in attendance finally moaned in unison. Actually, the moans tipped the scales at 51 percent because I joined in with them. Even the unicorn guy joined in. You know you've lost the crowd when the unicorn people are mocking you.

This was the exchange that defined the evening. One of the Christian apologists said to Horton, "I'll be praying for your salvation, Doctor."

"I appreciate that," said Dr. Horton, "but I'd rather you answer my question."

"Don't you want to be saved?"

"I want to be saved from the likes of you," said Horton, and most everyone laughed because the crowd was also frustrated the Christian apologist kept evading the question.

After the debate, I could hardly keep quiet.

"A God without wrath is a God Who tolerates the most unspeakable evil," I said, quoting someone but giving him no credit.

"A God of judgment is not inviting at all," said Miriam.

"You want a God Who doesn't judge?"

"Well, if I must have a god, that's the one I want," she said. Then she brought up a question posed by a member of Horton's team, who was a former-pastor-turned-atheist. "Why should Jesus be able to die for my sins, anyway? Why should His death apply to me?" And this from a former pastor of twenty years, verifying he had made the right career change.

"Yeah, why not King Kong?" asked Aaron. "I saw that on a bumper sticker once—King Kong died for my sins."

"And our three mouseketeers didn't really address it," said Evan.

"It's a long answer," I said.

"Give us the short one," said Evan.

"Because Jesus was sinless Man and infinite God. There."

"Great," said Evan. "Now give us a short one we can understand."

"Leviticus teaches the principle 'an eye for an eye,' a life for a life.[7] One human life equals one human life," I said. "So, if a sinless person who was only human could take your place, exchange his sinless life for your sinful one, that's the only life he could redeem because one human life equals one human life. Now, if he was sinless *and* his life had infinite value, then he could pay for the sins of anyone he wanted. But the only Being Whose life has infinite value is God. And there you have it. Christ is fully God and fully Man, so His life has infinite value. No one else is both infinite and sinless. Only He fits the bill. No one else is both

7   Leviticus 24:19-21

God and Man. That's why only His death can apply to you because *everyone else* is a sinner. Sorry, Buddha."

Evan and Aaron laughed at my Buddha line. Miriam did not.

Opting out of our post-debate conversation, Franky beelined to a table in the back to handle Horton's product, cash, and Square app; so Horton could spend the next sixty minutes shaking hands and signing books. Since getting to know him better, I could tell theology was not his preferred topic of debate. But he never felt debating the existence of God was that useful. He would have rather debated the foundation of morality and the implications of a universe that is strictly materialistic and, therefore, alone. Still, even on a topic that wasn't his preference, he was a formidable opponent.

"Congratulations," I said to Horton after the crowd had died down.

"Oh, was there a clear winner?"

"Are you serious?"

"Of course," he said. "You feel like you score some points along the way, but you don't really feel like you're persuading anyone. On the other team, anyway."

"You're not trying to convince Christians?"

"No, I'm trying to convince my fellow atheists to face the bleakness."

"Well, let's hope it worked."

"Thanks for coming," he said. "These debates fund our meetings."

"You mean the Unitarians are capitalists?"

"No, just socialists concerned about their carpeting."

I thanked him for the evening and gathered our carpooling troupe together.

As we drove home in Garry's car of the future, Evan, Franky, Garry, and I discussed the debate. To beat everyone to the punch, I stated loudly, "The Christians got slaughtered."

They all graciously agreed, except for Franky, who radiated glee.

"The atheists devoured them," he said. "Had them for dinner. Yup, yeah. All they had to do was sit back and burp. That was fantastic."

"Miriam seemed pleased with the victory," said Evan.

"I think she likes Horton," said Garry.

"She might," I said.

"How could you even tell that?" said Franky. "She hardly spoke."

"That's how I can tell," said Garry. "She just stood there, watching him talk to others. I recognize that because I love my wife like that."

"She barely knows him," said Franky.

"Okay," said Garry, knowing when to shut up.

CHAPTER 20

Franky soon became Horton's unofficial assistant, primarily because he hounded him about helping and would do whatever he wanted, gleefully running errands, laughing at everything Horton said, and feeding his ego in various other ways. Initially, Horton was hesitant, but Pam was tired of handling everything herself. Both were suspicious of professional agents, though they did consult Horton's lawyer with every contract. While training Franky, Pam discovered he had a knack for fielding calls—knowing what invitations to pursue and who to turn away, among other fine details—acting as Horton's own personal Radar O'Reilly. And because Horton and I had become friends and since Franky was my nephew, it just seemed like he fit.

It was during this period I sent a letter to Franky in a last-ditch effort to reason with him. I decided upon a letter because I knew it would have more impact than an email. Who gets handwritten letters anymore? In the interest of saving myself from emotional embarrassment, I won't print the entire letter here, but I will share the first couple of paragraphs and the very last paragraph with you because as the details of Franky's life unfold, I want you to know my heart toward him.

Dear Franky,

You probably remember the Ace Ventura *video I re-edited for you. You were about ten or twelve, double-digits for sure; and because* Ace Ventura *had so much foul language in it, your parents wouldn't let you watch it. But you really wanted to see it. So, with the caveman technology of two video recorders connected by cables that were only one notch above telepathy, I re-edited the movie and removed all the bits that were objectionable to your parents.*

Interestingly enough, editing Ace Ventura: Pet Detective *down to just forty minutes didn't hurt the storyline one bit. The plot was still intact, revealing the innate thinness of an extended skit. I hope you begin to see the plot for atheism is just as thin. Besides, I've spent way more time on this letter for you than I did re-editing that film. Not that I'm complaining, but I spent hours creating a version of that video you could enjoy because I love your mother. Because you're my nephew, I was there from the very beginning. It's because I love your mother that I love all the people she loves, and she loves you like crazy.*

Then I made some arguments against atheism and a plea for a better understanding of the Gospel. Those arguments were the bulk of the letter. I ended the letter with this:

What will it take to win your soul? Well, it will take a wise man; and without a hint of false humility, I am certain that is not me. All the arguments proposed in this little letter find their source in wiser men than myself. I give credit when I know the source (or remember it); but believe me, I'm just regurgitating better minds than my own, such as your own grandfather. However, I'm certain that even the wisest of the wise wouldn't be enough to win you back. Arguments only go so far. There is only One with enough wisdom, Whose words and actions have enough power to transform the human heart. That's really the issue at hand. You don't need a great argument. You need a great Savior. And One awaits. "Whoever comes to me I will never cast out."[8]

That next week, Franky picked me up and took me with him to a shooting range, though I don't think the letter had anything to do with his choice of venue. I had no interest in firearms—never have and probably never will—but he was insistent.

"You'll love it," he said.

"When did you develop an interest in guns?"

"A friend took me, and I loved the adrenaline rush it gave me. You'll see. Loved it. Just loved it."

This cooled my suspicions of his gun ownership because most people don't commit crimes with registered firearms.

The Los Angeles Gun Club was a cement behemoth, whose only windows were a line of darkened panes along the top of the building. The back, where we parked, was nothing but two-story concrete walls. Inside, it felt like a pawn shop, with assault weapons hanging behind glass counters filled with handguns. Posters of various cartoon assailants were plastered above the weapons—right next

---

to a big red sign reminding us not to point a loaded or unloaded gun at anyone.

There was an Asian guy behind the counter showing someone how to use a handgun. Another guy—a Caucasian with short, dark hair who looked like he was still in high school—helped Franky, who paid for our session. Since he didn't rent a gun, he didn't even have to show an ID.

The shooting range itself was a long row of stalls with numbers above each, much like a really long row of men's room stalls. Franky and I went to the door labeled Module 3; and once inside, he opened his shiny pistol case and explained everything about the weapon to me. Since I wasn't interested in guns, however, I didn't really retain the details, other than it was shiny and black and looked like a hitman's weapon from the movies.

He shot first to train me. Then I shot with those uncomfortable earmuffs on, imagining I was a dogsledder being attacked by a polar bear. I will admit, trying to hit the cartoon image of a bearded thug who held a female hostage by the shoulder ("Tactical Encounter No. 3") was fun—even though I shot the poor lady in the chin twice. Still, I didn't get the same kick out of it as Franky and never became a gun enthusiast. That was my first and last time at a shooting range, but it wouldn't be my last experience with one of Franky's guns.

Afterward, we went and had lunch. He never brought up the letter. And neither did I. Regretfully yours.

CHAPTER 21

When Horton's book sales shot out of the stratosphere, exceeding one million copies and eventually surpassing two million, he was making television appearances galore. He was set to appear on *The Late Late Show with Craig Kilborn,* so he asked Pam and me to tag along with him. Kilborn only hosted *The Late Late Show* for about five years, then basically retired because achieving his dream of hosting a late-night show "wasn't all it was cracked up to be."[9] I always find it refreshing when an entertainer tells us, in so many words, not to take entertainment so seriously.

Whenever Horton was on a show that had a lighter feel or outright comedy segments, he asked me to go over things with him beforehand. I was always willing to help because he made fun of the most popular kind of atheism, the kind of claptrap that said, "Because this life is all there is, that's what makes it more meaningful." Those are ideas I'm happy to satirize. This was our common bond, a disdain for optimistic atheism.

As usual, I'd jotted down ten jokes for him, and he read them over. Sometimes I'd shoot for twenty jokes, but it depended on the

---

9   Joe Flint, "Craig Kilborn Breaks his Silence," *Los Angeles Times,* June 06, 2010.

subject and how much time I could devote to it. He never memorized any of the jokes because we were both of the opinion that if a joke was any good, we'd remember it. His goal was to use the idea or the punchline in a conversation during the interview. It's true that everyone has a sense of humor, but not everyone can deliver a joke. Thankfully, Horton had good comedic timing. And for every ten jokes you write, only about one will be any good, anyway.

The green room for *The Late Late Show with Craig Kilborn* was large and comfortable with a long table of treats that I couldn't help going back to over and over again because I've always been a sucker for licorice in a tub.

"You're making a meal out of hors d'oeuvres," Pam said to me.

I shrugged and said, "I'm a snacker." Then between bites, I said to her, "So how you doing, old chum?"

"So, we're chums?"

"Absolutely," I said. "So, between you and me, old chum, what bothered you about Horton's dream?"

"Oh, that," she said.

"Yes, that. You left us hanging."

"I did," she said

"Why?"

"I don't want to be made fun of."

"I won't make fun of you."

She gave me an expression with her lips that implied, "Maybe."

"I don't think that's it, though," I said.

"Really?"

"You were shaken," I said. "Whatever you thought it meant, it shook you."

"You can't go by that," she said, "how I reacted emotionally."

"Oh, just tell me."

"You'll keep it between us?"

"Of course," I said. "We're chums."

She smirked at me but finally relented and said, "You remember his dream? Franky jumps off a cliff; and at the last second, it's Horton."

I nodded with food in my mouth.

She hesitated and then said, "Well, according to my understanding of the psychology of dreams, which is highly debatable and speculative—"

"Out with it already," I playfully interrupted.

"Okay, okay," she said. "A tragedy that is supposed to happen to Franky . . . will happen to Horton. Now, understand, this only reflects Horton's psychological makeup."

"You think Horton's aware of this?"

"Dreams are subconscious," she said.

"So, you think subconsciously, Horton feels like he's heading toward a tragedy with Franky?"

"Something like that."

By then, our plates were full.

The green room served all the guests; so when Phyllis Diller waltzed in, I was more than a little thrilled. And waltz in she did, with a sophistication that was not faked, forgoing those outfits that made her look like Big Bird puffing on a Tiparillo. At this stage of her career, she was past all that.

During my childhood, Phyllis Diller was the most famous female comedian in the country, cracking the soccer mom market before it existed, back when they were called housewives. In 2003, when this took place, she was very old, of course, and was out promoting a book on her life in comedy. I was glad to have a chance to speak with her and quote her back to herself—not that I quoted one of her jokes to her, but rather something else she said in an interview I had read in a book called *The Great Comedians Talk About Comedy*. She said that a comedian shouldn't be affected by the crowd, but "they should be affected by you. If they aren't, you're not strong enough to be up there in the white-hot spotlights."[10] That always stuck with me, so I told her so. Then she asked me some questions about myself; we discussed clean comedy; and she encouraged me to continue in that vein. She was thankful, gracious, and optimistic.

Horton's guest slot was in the show's third segment, the one usually reserved for some unknown comic like myself, authors, or other human-interest guests like the guy who can whistle the "William Tell Overture" through an orifice other than his mouth. But someone canceled—I forget who—so Horton was bumped up into the number two slot.

"My next guest tonight is the *New York Times* bestselling author . . . pause for ooohs and ahhhs . . . " But the crowd was basically silent, which was part of the gag as he continued, "Oh, really? What have

---

10   Larry Wilde, *The Great Comedians Talk About Comedy* (The Citadel Press, New York, 1968), 230.

you done lately? Maybe you didn't hear me right. *New York Times* bestselling author! And nary a picture in the book. His book, *The Honest Atheist,* is in stores now. Please welcome *the* honest atheist, Horton Murray."

The band played him out to cheers and Pavlov's applause sign.

Kilborn shook his hand and whispered something in his ear to make his guest feel comfortable. "I'm bored out of my mind," he probably said. "This job is killing me."

Horton nodded while smiling and took his seat.

Now the only reason Horton's interview is pertinent is because it was later used in the court trial. For that reason alone, I include it here

CHAPTER 22

"Welcome, Horton," said Kilborn. "May I call you Horton? Or should I call you Dr. Murray?"

"Horton's fine."

"It's a pleasure to have you on the program, though my grandmother would like to see you dead."

"Oh, is she religious?"

"No, just a psychopath."

Some laughter.

"What's the difference?" asked Horton.

Big laugh.

Horton could have coasted for the rest of the interview after that line. The crowd loved it, the *late* late-night crowds being even less religiously inclined than the earlier late-night crowds.

"So, give our audience a nutshell recap of your book in one sentence. This is late-night television, after all."

"Because we come from nothing, nothing has meaning."

"Boy, you can sure ruin a party."

"Not at all. I can be a lot of fun at a party. You know, as long as you don't tell me the party has some significance."

"Fun. Fun would be the point."

"I'm all for fun. Eat, drink, and be merry; for tomorrow is nothing."

"Yeah, see, that's the kind of conversation-stopper I'm talkin' about."

"Well, that's the point," Horton said. "We need to be honest about where this worldview leads."

"What would you call a worldview that's entire point is 'girls just want to have fun'?"

"Shallow."

That received a big laugh and an applause break.

Kilborn pretended to write down some notes on a pad, reciting back to himself, "Don't be shallow. Okay. Got it." Then he looked back at Horton and said, "Your book has sold over 1.5 million copies. That's a lot of unbelief."

"Thank you, but the Bible is still the bestselling book every year."

"Is that true?"

"Yes."

"Now, how do you happen to know that fact?"

"One of my best friends is an evangelical Christian."

In the green room, Pam said to me, "Like he has more than one."

"Sounds like a sitcom in the making," said Kilborn.

"He's also a standup comedian—Sam Seitz."

Pam punched me in the arm as we watched.

"Why does that name sound familiar?" asked Kilborn.

"He's been on *The Tonight Show* a few times."

"Oh . . . I don't usually get a chance to watch because, you know, I'm working on this little thing called *The Late Late Show*."

Then the show went to a commercial break. The show wasn't taped live; but it was taped in real-time, so it felt live. I always intended to ask Horton what they spoke about during the break but, regretfully, never did.

After welcoming everyone back and reintroducing his guest, Kilborn said, "You know what I love about your book, worth the price alone, is that opening chapter on the history of atheism."

"Thank you."

"Would it be fair to say you find your own beliefs disturbing?"

"To believe that when we die, we cease to exist is rightfully a disturbing thought. To claim, as some do, that it's really nothing to worry about because it's just part of life is either self-deceptive or disingenuous. Death is not part of life. That's a ridiculous statement. Death ends life. So, to be a true atheist—an honest atheist—you have to have a measure of despair. You know, until you arrive at the party."

He received an okay laugh with that one. Even Kilborn genuinely laughed.

"I take it back," said Kilborn. "If I ever have a party, you're invited. And you can bring one atheist friend, living or dead. Who would it be?"

"Nietzsche."

"Great mustache. Why Nietzsche?"

"I'd like to argue with him."

"Lemme guess. About *nothing*?"

"Not at all. About morality. Though he called himself an immoralist . . . "

"They make the best dates, by the way."

Horton had been coached enough to wait for the laughter to die down before he continued, "Even as an immoralist, Nietzsche did make a moral argument. And all moral imperatives imply God."

"There are no absolutes?" said Kilborn.

"There are no moral absolutes, except for when someone ticks me off."

Horton managed to find the perfect time to interject one of the jokes I'd supplied him, and I held up my arms in a victory pose as the crowd laughed.

"Does that mean life only has meaning when you're driving?"

"Something like that," said Horton.

"You know what intrigues me about you?" asked Kilborn. "You rile both the left and the right. Why do you think that is?"

"I think I rile up the right because I don't believe in God. And I rile up the left because I maintain that social-political arguments for morality are vapid."

"You should probably define 'vapid' for us. This is a late-night talk show."

"Airy, lightweight."

"There you go." Then Kilborn looked into the camera and addressed the viewers. "Thanks for staying up late with us. Sleep in. It's not like anything you have to do tomorrow matters. Right, Horton? Horton Murray, ladies and gentlemen!"

Applause.

He held up the book. "*The Honest Atheist.* We'll be right back!"

CHAPTER 23

Such appearances usually gave Horton an adrenaline rush, so we drove over to Roscoe's House of Chicken and Waffles, where he could counteract the adrenaline rush with a sugar crash.

"Great job tonight," I said. "You always do well in your interviews."

"I can tell you his secret," said Pam.

"Tell me."

"Not caring," she said.

I laughed.

"No, really," she said.

"She knows me too well," said Horton.

"He doesn't think anything in life has real significance," she said. "How can he get nervous about anything?"

"Is that it—your secret?"

"It is, actually," he said. "I wouldn't call it a secret, but I don't put too much stock in anything. Never take it all very seriously, you know. I didn't know the book would become a bestseller. I thought I'd be a journalist the rest of my life."

"Instead of the celebrity author he has become," said Pam. "Admit it. You enjoy it."

"I do. I like the distraction. Makes life move very fast."

"You'd think if you were heading toward nonexistence, you'd want life to move slower," I said.

"Fair point," said Horton.

"What about death?"

"Death is the easy part," he said. "You're a comedian. You should know that."

"Dying is easy. Comedy is hard," I said, quoting an old adage.

"Yes," he said. "You die; so what? You won't remember your troubles. You won't know you existed. But living, knowing it all means nothing . . . that can be unbearable at times."

"I hate when he talks like that," said Pam. "That's why I can't finish his book."

Horton and I often had knotty discussions, but it was rare that he displayed any vulnerability. This was a rare occasion. He was always a little more at ease when Pam was around.

"I think one of the reasons your book sold so well is that there is a certain courage in living life as you do," I said.

"I don't really live it. I just write about it."

At the time, I didn't really think about this statement but later realized it was a kind of portent, as was the moment a second later when Franky invaded our meal by calling and berating Horton for not inviting him to the taping. Franky was so upset, Pam and I could hear every word through Horton's cell.

"You do enough during the day," Horton said. "It wouldn't be fair for you to spend your evenings with me."

"Like Miriam?" asked Franky.

"Miriam didn't come."

"Oh."

"There's nothing going on with Miriam and me," said Horton. "She's a decade or more younger than I am, Franky. She doesn't want an old fart like me."

"She doesn't?"

"She wants nothing to do with me."

"That's not how it seems to me," said Franky.

"Well, that's the way it is," said Horton.

After Horton hung up, I asked him if that was true.

"The kid's so insecure," he said.

"So, something *is* going on with Miriam?"

"Don't you start," he said.

"What? What's the big deal?"

He wouldn't answer me, so I looked at Pam.

"He won't say anything to me, either," she said.

"I tell you what," said Horton. "I'll announce it at my birthday."

"Announce what?" asked Pam.

"That is the question," said Horton.

"Sometimes, I dislike your mysterious side," she said.

"Well, I won't miss that birthday party," I said.

"Depends on who's handling the guest list," said Horton.

"Man, he's on fire," I said to Pam.

"He's letting your joke go to his head."

"It's just a birthday," said Horton. "It doesn't mean anything."

"You really live by your book title, don't you?"

"I live by my premise," he said, not knowing his premise was about to be tested in an unthinkable way.

CHAPTER 24

Horton looked at his watch, and it was one of those moments on the timeline of his life he would never forget because he considered making an alternative decision. Horton was supposed to meet my wife and me; Evan and his latest, long-term relationship that would soon end; and Aaron Belle and his wife, Dawn, at Twin Palms to celebrate his birthday. I was hoping Franky wouldn't tag along, but he was difficult to shake. It turns out, Franky had planned his own little surprise for Horton, which Miriam was agreeable enough to help him with, to her everlasting regret.

Horton didn't think whatever Franky had in mind would take long since Franky had moved to Eagle Rock himself and wasn't far away. Horton was intrigued enough to make the stop; but first, he had to run an errand for Miriam that she dropped on him at the last second. He had to stop at a local grocery to pick up a cake she had ordered. This was also the night Horton was going to make his announcement, which Pam and I assumed had something to do with his relationship with Miriam, at his small and intimate birthday dinner.

This is the version of the events relayed to me by Horton Murray of that day:

Horton received a call from Franky, who said, "Isn't today your birthday? Because I've got a surprise for you."

"Okay," said Horton, who made the mistake of not wanting to hurt Franky's feelings.

"You'll have to come over, but it'll be worth it."

"Can't you just bring it to me?"

"I'm afraid I can't. But believe me, it'll be worth it."

"So, I heard," said Horton, trying to sound good-natured about the whole thing. That's when he looked at his watch. The odd thing is he doesn't even remember the time.

When Horton arrived, Franky was sitting in his car, grinning like someone sitting on a plate of tacks, teeth forced across his face. He waved Horton over. Franky held up a bottle, toasting Horton; so Horton opened the passenger door, sat down, and took the bottle.

"Happy birthday!"

"Thank you," said Horton, and they clinked bottle tips.

"I want you to know," said Franky, "you've been the most influential person in my life." This is usually taken as a compliment and not as something you'd regret.

"Here's to you on my birthday," said Horton.

That's when Franky started the car.

"What are we doing?" asked Horton.

"The surprise isn't here," said Franky. "Don't worry. Miriam's in on this."

"She is?"

"I swear," said Franky, and Horton couldn't help believing him because of the conviction in his voice. Come to find out, it was true in one sense.

"Hey, my phone's dead," said Franky. "Let me use your GPS." Horton handed Franky his phone, usually an inconsequential act, but in this case, one with a harrowing aftermath, making Horton replay this moment over and over again in his mind asking those useless what-if questions of himself.

During the drive, Franky talked incessantly but only to get Horton to talk. And being a talker, Horton talked—especially when Franky broached the topic of whether or not marriage was an outdated concept. Horton went to town on that one; and the next thing he knew, Franky pulled over to the side of the road.

"We're almost there," said Franky. "Put this on." And he handed Horton a black cloth blindfold.

"Are you serious?" asked Horton.

"Deadly," said Franky.

Horton shook his head in resignation and put on the blindfold.

"I tested it, so I know you can't cheat," said Franky. "It won't be a minute."

The ride didn't continue on regular streets for much longer. Horton felt the car turn, and then it continued to twist and wind in unusual ways, like Franky was circling an unusually large parking lot with bumpy patches at intervals. Minutes later, the car bounced along on severely potholed pavement. Then it came to a stop.

"Okay, hold on just a moment," said Franky. "Almost ready. Give me a couple minutes. Now, don't peek, or you'll ruin it."

Then Franky jumped out of the car, went to the trunk, popped it open, and removed something like a giant sack of potatoes. Horton listened to Franky traipse along the pavement and grunt to heave whatever it was onto wherever he lifted it. For a moment—or maybe it was minutes—Horton didn't hear anything. He was taken up in the mystery of this birthday surprise against his own better judgment.

Finally, he heard Franky walk back to the car and open the door.

CHAPTER 25

Horton asked, "Can I remove it now?"

"Yup, yeah," said Franky.

Horton removed the blindfold and found himself at the Los Angeles Rail Yard in a ghost yard of old equipment.

"A boxcar?" asked Horton.

"The surprise is in there," said Franky, nodding forcefully in a way that intrigued Horton. So, he took the lead, climbed out of the vehicle, and marched over to the boxcar. In front of the steel and corrugated open sliding door, he looked at Franky, who gave him a "welcome to my world" grin, peaking with carved-out dimples. Then Horton looked back at the boxcar, wondering what he was getting himself into with the kind of curiosity that kills house pets. With that, he grabbed the side of the door channel, put his foot on the bottom door track, and pulled himself up.

Once inside, it took a moment for his eyes to adjust. The first thing Horton saw was Miriam lying comatose with her arms bound at the wrists and pulled outward and her legs bound at the ankles also pulled outward. Only her bra and underwear remained as the ropes wrenched her into a human X. She had clearly been drugged.

The second thing Horton noticed was a gaping hole in the upper left-hand corner of the boxcar that let in just enough light to make things eerie. When he turned his head, he saw Franky smiling like this was the best surprise in the world.

"I got her for you," said Franky, grinning like this was Horton's deepest birthday wish.

Not sure whether revealing the fact he was already in an intimate relationship with Miriam would make things better or worse, all Horton could think of to say was, "What?"

"Miriam. She's all yours. Happy birthday!"

"What do you mean she's all mine?"

"To rape."

"You think I would just rape her?"

"Well, why not? You said as much. Let's stop just talking about things."

It was at this point Horton realized things were even bleaker than he could have imagined because Franky was holding a shiny black handgun at his side. Initially mesmerized by the surroundings, he had failed to notice Franky smuggle it at his side. Horton knew then that reasoning with Franky wouldn't work. He had to think of some other way to get him and Miriam out of this nightmare.

"I guess I gave her a little too much," said Franky, as Miriam's eyes slowly opened.

"Horton?" she asked with a dry and hoarse throat.

She still didn't have the energy to scream out as she became aware of her bindings and mostly naked state. But resentment filled her face, and she said, "Franky, you—"

"It's not just me, Miriam," Franky said, pronouncing her name with a sneer. "It's me and Horton."

Miriam looked at Horton; and he went pale because he knew Franky was looking at him, too, and he didn't want Franky to see any dissent on his face.

"Why?" croaked Miriam.

"Because we can," Franky said proudly.

"Franky got you for me as a birthday gift," said Horton with a tone and expression he hoped communicated to her in the subtext they were dealing with a madman. If nothing else, he hoped she saw it in his eyes: *I'll get you out of this.*

Franky turned to Horton and said, "We can get away with this. You know how many bodies are dumped in the Mojave Desert and never found? And even when they're found, the cases are usually so cold they stay that way. We can do this."

From that point on, it was clear to him that whatever Franky had planned, he was going to kill Miriam. Horton didn't understand why at this point, but he had a feeling Franky was being insincere in some way. But how could that be? After all, he had kidnapped her—that seemed pretty sincere. Still, there it was in the back of his mind: *I think he's going to kill us both.*

"I thought she was just for me?"

"I'll let you go first; but afterward, I'm going, too. I mean, she is hot."

"How did you get her here?"

"I said you were coming over, that I had planned a little surprise party with some of your journalist acquaintances. There were no acquaintances, of course. But there was a cake—to delay you. Not for the party like she thought, but so I could get to her first. 'Let's have a drink before they get here.' She fell for it, and I put her in the trunk. She was there the whole time you were in my car."

Franky had spiked Miriam's drink with Liquid-X—the date rape drug—known in mobster days as a Mickey Finn and less commonly known today as gamma-hydroxybutyric acid.

"I think deep down, she likes you."

"You think she likes me?" asked Horton.

"I do."

"Well, she's here. Let's ask her."

Franky walked over to Miriam, knelt down, poked her belly gently with the pistol's barrel, and said, "Well?"

Now Horton could really hear it in his voice—Franky wanted to kill her.

If he wanted to get Miriam out of there alive, he knew he had to get the jump on Franky.

CHAPTER 26

Miriam said, calmly and slowly, "Please, Franky, please don't do this."

Rocking to his knees, he leaned over, putting his nose to her hair and sniffing like he was taking in his mother's favorite casserole, then added, "You smell great. Everything's heightened. You know why? We're doing it—actually living out a premise most people are too afraid to live out. You see, we're not just talking about doing it. We're doing it."

Horton said, "I'm not sure these conditions are, well, conducive, if you know what I mean."

"There's the faint heart I was waiting for," said Franky.

"This is a challenge, I take it?" asked Horton, trying to sound cool and smooth.

"Maybe."

"You don't catch my meaning, Franky. I'm not into someone else watching."

"Well, I'm the one with the gun."

"Are you threatening me?"

"No," said Franky as he put the handgun to Miriam's temple. "I'm threatening her. You got some feelings for her, Doc?"

"Please don't, Franky," said Miriam with the kind of fear that chokes vocal cords.

Horton's instincts had told him Franky was planning to kill them both. Now he was sure of it.

"I don't think you have the stomach for your own ideas," said Franky, pressing the gun barrel tight to Miriam's head. Then he sprung to his feet and took several steps away from her. "Pick up her clothes and throw them in that corner."

Looking for any opportunity to buy time, Horton complied. But then Franky's commands became more and more severe as he instructed Horton to forcefully remove Miriam's remaining undergarments—so much so that Miriam repeatedly said, "You're vile. You're just so vile." Horton knew she was speaking to Franky; but at the same time, he felt the words bounce off Franky and land on him, the instrument of Franky's grotesque psyche. During this cirque du cruelty, Horton wanted to whisper something reassuring to Miriam but decided against it, fearing Franky's reaction if overheard. Horton kept thinking, *I have to get closer to him somehow.* He feared if he didn't try to jump him soon, they were both dead.

"Now put your face to her hand," ordered Franky as he waved the gun.

"What?"

"I said put your face to her hand."

"Okay, okay," said Horton.

"Scratch his face," Franky said to Miriam.

Miriam could only mouth the word "please" without sound, but Franky was unmoved.

"Scratch!" he screamed. "Scratch like you're buried alive!"

And she did. She scratched Horton's face like she was in a dark, wooden casket under the ground; and maybe, in her irrational panic, she thought she could split the wood with her fingernails and dig herself out. At the end of it, Horton's face was a bloody mess, like a cat in a gunnysack had been placed over his head. Feeling responsible for the situation, he had kept his face there until she stopped. Even Horton would later describe this as an act of penance, which has always baffled him, a man who claimed no religious impulse whatsoever.

"Why are you doing this, Franky?" asked Miriam, tears covering her cheeks, burning off the grime that dusted her face.

"I am sick of inconsistent people," said Franky. "Nothing is right, and nothing is wrong. There are no absolutes. People will say it. But no one will live it. It's not just inconsistent. It's hypocrisy."

"But you do, is that it, Franky?" asked Horton, as he prepared to spring toward his psycho protégé at the most opportune moment. But he still wasn't close enough.

"I'm going to leave here alive; and one day, I'm going to write about what really happened," said Franky. "One day, the world will see that someone had the courage to live it." He took a menacing step closer to Miriam, then suddenly changed his demeanor. "Okay, that's enough fun for me. Thanks for cooperating, guys. Really. But now it's time." He lowered the weapon and walked toward the door. "Tell you what I'm gonna do. I'm gonna honor your request, Doc.

I'll give you a few minutes alone with her. When I come back, you know what I better find."

Without taking his eyes off Horton, he slid the boxcar door open and said, "I'll be right out here. I've disabled the door, by the way; so you can't lock it from the inside."

Then he jumped down and pulled it shut.

CHAPTER 27

Horton felt a small surge of hope that maybe this would give them an opportunity to escape.

"Leave her tied up," Franky said as he pounded on the door. "Hear me?"

Horton yelled yes through the door.

"He's got my phone," Horton said in realization.

"I don't want to die," said Miriam.

"That's not gonna happen," he said while working at the nylon ropes that bound her. "I promise."

"What will you do?"

"I'll jump him—as soon as he's within arm's length."

"Okay," she said with uncertainty.

Unwilling to admit he was baffled by the constrictor knot, he kept pulling at it until the skin on his thumbs and index fingers blistered. He masked his defeat with a pep talk.

"We're gonna get out of here and make our announcement. I might even shout it from some rooftops. I don't care who knows anymore. Why restrict it to a select group of friends? Let's tell strangers. Why not? That parent-teacher thing is coming up. Let's announce it there, too. Then we'll take Charlotte to Disneyland. Yes, Disneyland. You see what I'm willing to do for you? Disneyland." He stopped tussling with the ropes; and though he didn't believe in the soul, he tried to look into her being through her eyes. "You've changed everything for me, you know. Everything."

"Me, too."

Then in frustration, he admitted, "I can't get these loose."

"It's okay. You can cut them off later." She gave a weak smile that didn't convince either one of them.

"Okay, then," he said, disappointed in his own blandness of expression, having nothing significant to say, no appropriate quote for the moment but only the workaday phrase: "This is it."

"What do you think he's gonna do when he sees you haven't raped me?"

"I really don't think he expects me to."

"You don't?"

"I think he's trying to prove a point, among other things." Using his thumbs, he wiped the tears from her cheeks and said, "I'm so sorry this is happening to you."

With that, Horton pounded on the boxcar door, two good whacks with his palm. The door skittered open. Franky looked in and said, "Move back," while waving the pistol like an overzealous traffic cop. One upward pull with his left arm and a lunge with his right leg showed that he'd cased the railcar enough to skillfully maneuver in and out of its carcass.

Now he was standing at the edge of the opening, shaking his head while looking at Miriam. "I knew you didn't have it in ya, Doc," he said. "But you didn't have to rape her, did ya? Because you two got something goin' on."

Horton didn't answer.

Franky reached in his pocket, pulled out Horton's cell phone, and tossed it to him.

Horton caught it.

"What's this for?" he asked and then returned the phone to his back pocket so his hands would be free. In that moment, Horton knew it like never before—he was alone in the world. Nothing in the universe existed outside of this boxcar and the gun in Franky's hand.

Franky looked at his watch, and Horton felt he had no choice but to lunge at the man right then, so he fired his body toward Franky. Having no idea what he was doing and operating only on instinct and adrenaline, Horton grabbed at the gun with his right hand and twisted it toward the right because that was his strong hand. Franky's was the same, so he pushed it back toward Horton and in doing so, pulled the trigger.

The bullet hit Miriam in the face, shocking both men into a frozen stillness.

She was manifestly dead, her forehead hanging open. Horton's adrenaline spiked, and he ripped the gun away with almost supernatural strength, then staggered a few steps back.

He pointed the barrel at Franky's chest.

"No, no, no!" cried Franky, and Horton shot him twice.

Franky hit the floor. It was that sack of potatoes sound again.

As the ringing in his ears slowly faded, he heard a demanding voice. "Police! This is the police! Throw down your weapon and come out with your hands up!"

Horton looked over and realized the boxcar door had been left open. The officer pointing his weapon at Horton had just seen him shoot Franky. Horton dropped the gun and put his hands up. There were two squad cars parked outside the railroad car.

Horton was treated as the primary suspect, cooperating and answering all the questions he was asked while handcuffed. One of the cops, who had introduced himself as Officer Bellmeyer, asked Horton while examining his license, "So, you're Horton Murray? The author?"

"Yes."

"Who called the police?" asked the other officer named Maxwell.

"Not me," said Horton. "He took our phones."

"But we found your phone on you," said Officer Maxwell.

"He gave it back to me right before I shot him," said Horton, realizing how stupid that sounded.

"It was a male named Franky who made the call," said Officer Maxwell. "Whispering."

"Five-four-nine-six. That's not you?" asked Officer Bellmeyer.

"That's Franky's number," said Horton.

"The dead guy?"

"Yeah."

"Hmmm," said Officer Maxwell.

At this point, another squad car with two officers and an unmarked car with a detective rolled into the scene.

"Well," said Officer Bellmeyer to himself, "just for a moment." With that, he leaned over and released the handcuffs from Horton. As Horton rubbed his wrists, the cop handed him a pen and pad and said, "Can you make it out to Melvin?"

Horton didn't realize initially what the man was asking for; but after a few moments, it dawned on him.

"You serious?" he said.

"Absolutely," replied Officer Bellmeyer. "I loved your book."

So, Horton wrote: *To Melvin—I wish we could have met under different circumstances. Yours Truly, Horton Murray.*

He didn't know, of course, this would later be used against him at his trial along with a transcript of *The Late Late Show with Craig Kilborn* to argue that Horton didn't believe murder or rape were necessarily wrong. There are things you can say during comedic repartee that don't sound funny on a transcript read in a courtroom. But the most damning evidence against him, of course, was that a police officer saw him shoot Franky in the chest while Franky pled for his life.

Franky had died instantly; but before he did, he had also made sure Horton Murray was doomed.

CHAPTER 28

Pam and I stood in the driveway as the police searched Horton's place, hoping to fetch a secret life from the jaws of suburbia. We huddled together, whispering like co-conspirators of some underground resistance, still believing in his innocence until proven otherwise, though fearful to verbalize this publicly. Nevertheless, Pam was troubled by what she had heard so far—that even after Franky had pled for him not to shoot, Horton shot him twice.

"If an officer wouldn't have seen it, I still wouldn't believe it," she said. "And I can't go down the police conspiracy angle because . . . why? That makes no sense. None of this makes any sense. My brother shot his . . . what do we call her? Love interest? And his assistant? It's unthinkable."

"It was self-defense," I said.

She lowered her eyes at me, using the same spoon to dish up both empathy and condescension. I wanted to tell her something wasn't right about Franky; but all I had was a gut feeling, nothing substantial besides a vaguely haunting mirage of the Los Padres National Forest. All I knew was that if Horton shot Franky, he probably had good reason. But I couldn't say it aloud because it sounded horrible to say. What I did say was, "Franky had a thing for Miriam."

"I had my suspicions," said Pam. "The looks he gave when she called. I could tell it bothered him when Horton talked to her, but . . . I can't imagine he'd . . . doesn't matter . . . His life is over."

And I knew she meant her brother.

"Boy, pessimism's a family trait, I guess.

She shrugged with the mournful sulk of someone facing the truth.

"You can't talk like that," I said. "He hasn't even been charged yet."

"He's in jail."

"They're detaining him."

"He's never been to jail in his life."

"We'll get him through this," I assured her.

She looked off into the sky, letting a slight breeze snap her hair against her face and said, "My brother's thinking has come back to bite him."

"Ideas have consequences, and that's all your brother's guilty of. He didn't force Franky's hand."

"No. His ideas did."

"Happy thoughts," I said. "Think happy thoughts."

In the back of the open garage, an officer yelled, "I got something."

There was a commotion as multiple officers swarmed into Horton's garage, where some crime photographer was snapping shots near the back. Following the proper documentation and bagging, the herd of officers split a path as someone carried the newfound evidence out of the garage with their right arm extended like the contents were either holy or contagious. I could see it in his eyes as he passed—this was a payload find. Hidden behind a ramshackle wall of boxes filled with Horton's best-selling book, they uncovered a toolbox containing rope, a gun case, and most damning of all—a Polaroid photo of Syd Hawkins, dead, with that cryptic homemade sign on her lap: *The Grand Experiment.*

Pam buried her head in my shoulder and cried.

I let her cry for a bit, but then I took her by the shoulders and said, "Look at me. This doesn't mean anything. You know why?"

She knew.

"I want you to say it," I said.

She nodded.

"C'mon now," I said.

She took a tissue from her pocket, breezed the contents of her nose into it, and took a deep breath because that's what you do when the universe rearranges itself while you just stand there. Then she looked at me and said, "Because Franky was here all the time."

"That's right," I said. "Franky had the run of the place."

"You believe my brother, don't you?" she asked with a tinge of pleading in her voice.

"Of course, I do."

And there was a glint of hope in her eyes, just enough to stop the world from shuffling around any more items.

CHAPTER 29

When I came across Atheists for Human Rights, I knew I had found what I was looking for; an organization that could help. A woman named Mary Alena Hagen founded the group, which is located in what she herself deemed "the Hub of Atheism," a nice, little geodesic dome in Minneapolis, Minnesota, that houses the organization's law offices, meeting room, library, and video studios. The hub of atheism is in Minneapolis. Who knew?

She wanted to call it The Center for Atheism; but according to city ordinances, she didn't have enough square footage to be the center. The zoning people said a "center" has specific criteria. So, it's a hub instead. But she can still dream.

Mary Alena, another former Catholic who abandoned her faith over forty years ago after personal introspection, answered the phone herself. I didn't ask her age, but her voice crackled in that warm way elderly voices often do.

"I understand you take cases pro bono in the interests of atheism?" I said.

"Yes, I do," she said.

"I'm calling about Horton Murray's case."

She paused, and I could almost hear her thoughts racing.

"I'm familiar with his case," she said.

"He's innocent."

"That's too bad because he's already been convicted."

"This is for his appeal," I said.

During the trial, Horton's defense team had him explain the events in his own words; then the prosecution proceeded to unravel his testimony with various bits of evidence, which Mary Alena quickly reminded me of.

"Officer Maxwell saw him shoot Franky," she said. "Point blank."

"He admitted he didn't see anything prior. His observation of the shooting lacks context."

"The use of lethal force alone is not what convicted him. It was that with everything else, which was plenty."

"Nothing was beyond doubt."

"His DNA was found in the body of the victim. That's indisputable."

"They were developing a relationship. He had spent the night with her—for the first time—right before Franky called him."

"His fingerprints were on the weapon."

"So were Franky's. There was a struggle for the gun."

"Yet gun residue was only found on Murray's hand."

"His hands were on top of Franky's. Then, because he feared for his life, he gained control of the weapon and shot Franky."

"Twice," she said with great emphasis, which shut me up for a moment. "The ropes were from Murray's own garage," she added.

"Well," I said, trying to regain conviction and composure, "Franky was his lackey and had access to his home—to everything, really. Franky handled Horton's calendar."

"And I suppose that's how the gun case ended up there, too?"

"Yes," I said. "He was framed. They still don't know where the gun came from. And Franky owned guns."

"But the murder weapon wasn't his."

"Yeah, the gun's still a mystery," I conceded. "But Horton was not known as a gun enthusiast."

"He only had to be enthusiastic once," she said. I didn't know what to say to that, but didn't have to because she immediately followed it up with another question: "So how do you explain the manuscript?"

One of the motives presented at the trial was that Horton killed Franky because the student was about to eclipse the teacher, so to speak. They had found an unpublished manuscript Franky had supposedly written that was dedicated to Horton. The problem was they had found the same manuscript on Horton's laptop, except it was written by him. That was circumstantial until they found the emails. The emails condemned Horton in everyone's eyes, except for Aaron, Pam, and me—we were still stubbornly holding to his innocence.

"And the emails?" asked Mary Alena.

"Those I can't explain."

"Yes, neither could the defense."

They had found email exchanges between Horton and Franky, which sounded like Franky had been working on a writing project— the said manuscript. In the emails, he told Horton he had dedicated the book to him and couldn't wait for him to read it. Since Horton had a book deal for which he'd already received the advance, it was argued he needed a book. They made it sound like he was desperate for a hot idea and had decided to nab Franky's book and do away with him. In reality, Horton's book hadn't been sent to the publisher yet. He wasn't even working with an editor yet. *The Amoral Universe* was still being shaped; so unfortunately, no one else had laid eyes on it other than his weaselly assistant Franky.

"But it's not how it looks," I said, knowing my hope in his innocence was more emotional than rational.

"But can you see how it looks?" she asked. "Can you understand why he was convicted of double homicide and rape?"

The D.A. had also just charged him with the murder and rape of Syd Hawkins, tying him to the scene with the Polaroid from his garage.

"I understand why," I said, "but it's not the truth."

"What was your name again?"

"Sam Seitz."

"Your testimony helped convict him."

"Well, I had to answer yes that we discussed a hypothetical rape."

"That he said, point blank, he would be willing to commit. Along with murder. Of the victim."

"It was a philosophical discussion."

"More than one person testified to hearing this."

"I know. I was there. But it was a joke."

"That was an unfortunate joke," she said. "And to top it off, his philosophy of life—if one can call it that—is that morality doesn't exist. It's a fabrication, he claims. And in the discussion at the restaurant, he said you could rape or murder, and it wouldn't be wrong morally as long as you could get away with it."

"It was a discussion. That doesn't make him a murderer."

"No, the evidence does."

"Why would he rape a woman he was having a relationship with? Forensics can't tell us what kind of sex they had, only that they'd had sex."

"His DNA was all over her torn bra and underwear, her clothes, her skin, under her fingernails," Mary Alena pointed out.

"But there wasn't any trauma to the body."

"She was drugged, in which case body trauma during rape is lessened, if not eliminated altogether. And there *was* body trauma—bruising and welts around her arms and legs from the ropes. And from everything that was ripped from her body—her undergarments."

"Which he did at gunpoint," I said.

"That's according to Horton alone, who had scratch marks from her fingernails on his face."

"It was all coerced."

"Again, according to him," said Mary Alena. "Besides, no one could verify their relationship."

"It was implied."

"But it wasn't stated."

"No."

"The prosecution made the case that Horton was obsessed with her," Mary Alena said.

"That's not hard evidence," I said, hoping some would turn up leading the other way and soon.

"Not hard evidence, I know, but even her daughter couldn't confirm their relationship."

"I think she was protecting her daughter until she knew it was serious."

"Well," said Mary Alena, "that's nice to know, but his sister couldn't confirm it either. All she confirmed was they spoke on the phone. She never saw them together. She couldn't verify it was mutual. And he never admitted even to his own sister that it was. But none of that's the real problem for me."

I knew it was coming. I even suspected it might be the first thing she brought up because it was the only thing that introduced doubt in my own mind.

"What's the real problem?" I asked, already knowing the answer.

"The Polaroid of the dead girl."

"Okay, they find the Polaroid, why not the camera? I mean, if he's going to start raping and killing women, taking souvenir photographs afterward, why not keep the camera?"

"You have an answer for everything," said Mary Alena. "You should have been on his defense team."

"I am."

She gave a slight snort, so I decided to switch tactics in the hopes of securing her help.

CHAPTER 30

"You're an atheist, right?" I said. "Now, I don't want to assume anything about your beliefs; but my assumption is that you, as an atheist, believe when we die, that's it—nothingness."

"When you're dead, you're dead," she said. "Your brain ceases to function."

"Okay. Here's an innocent man who is going to spend the rest of his life in prison, all because a fan of his bestselling book wanted to show him his own hypocrisy. Fine. He's a hypocrite, but he's not a killer. If this life is all he has, you can save it for him."

"His book wasn't helpful either," she said. "It really conspired against him."

"I get that."

"The man constantly argues against all moral standards," she emphasized.

Horton's book was unique among books on atheism because he was extremely hard on fellow atheists who argued for any type of morality—figures like Peter Singer who argued that interests larger than the individual show us there is a morality that is "somehow universal." According to Horton, "somehow" isn't an argument but "an emotional appeal at worst, an assumption at best."

Even though Horton was a bestselling author who opened the door for other mass-market books on atheism, he wasn't popular among the famous atheists who succeeded him. He was always an outlier, which is one of the reasons I liked him so much. He made a case for true amorality over and against the standard atheistic arguments for morality, which neither one of us ever found convincing.

Many atheists answered the need for moral values by contending science provided a moral basis for human flourishing, the argument that heavily influenced Miriam. But Horton wrote that "science can never provide us with an ought."

He explained this in his book:

> We can arbitrarily assign value to things, but that doesn't make them facts. Certainly, all sentient beings suffer more than insects or rocks; but if one uses this to adamantly argue pleasure is therefore a proven good, the assigned value to pleasure is still arbitrary. It is not a proven good. Even if it's measured in the brain, to assign a particular value to the measurement is still arbitrary. Science simply does not give us morality, let alone absolute morality.

> When my fellow atheists do not admit to the premise that nothing matters in a random universe, they play into the hands of religious demagogues who say, "You see? They can't help but care because the laws of God are written upon their hearts." It's better to admit the truth. It's better to be an honest atheist, who

says, "There is nothing in the universe that produces a standard morality among our species."

This was used against him at his trial, in order to show his mindset.

"I think Horton's ideas about the universe are profoundly wrong," I said to Mary Alena, "but I don't believe he is the monster he is portrayed to be in the press. He was set up by a very crafty zealot—"

"Who called 911 and claimed to be one of the victims."

"But don't you see?" I said. "That's why he called 911—to give the impression of innocence."

"I hate to tell you this, but it worked."

"It was a lie. People bought a lie."

"This is an issue that has always troubled me," she said. "If Franky was the murderer, why would he call 911 before he killed them? Why not after?"

"Well, he didn't end up killing both of them," I said. "His plan went awry. And I think that's why he called first. On the chance that things went south, he wanted to make sure he looked innocent. Plus, that 911 call painted him as the victim from the get-go."

"Pure speculation."

"Well, we can't piece together all his reasoning. He's dead."

"This conjecture will get us nowhere," she said. "What about the letter they found on his laptop? You think it was a forgery?"

"Of course. It detailed the crime in a way that was way too contrived. Franky took an old letter that Horton wrote and modified it. That's why the details of the crime are spread throughout and oddly worded."

"But that wasn't proven."

"No," I said with barely any air left in my lungs.

"And the email exchanges between them where Horton basically says he wants to rape Miriam?"

"I can't explain those," I said, "but I know he didn't write them."

"They came from his IP address. From his laptop."

"I know."

"You have to face everything you're up against," she said and then recited her list like she was watching the cardboard disk in a View-Master, one horrific scene after another snapping by: "the 911 call from Franky pleading for help; two dead bodies; the witness; Murray's fingerprints on the weapon; gun residue on his hands alone; his DNA inside her; his DNA all over her undergarments; his DNA under her fingernails; the scratches on his face; the email exchanges; the letter forecasting the crime; the stolen manuscript; and to top it all off, a Polaroid of another murder victim found on his premises. That's quite a list to overcome."

"I realize that."

"Look, I appreciate your sincerity. I am convinced you believe he's innocent. And I would like him to be innocent because it hurts the profile of atheism. But you have to bring me one solid thing I can build upon. If you can do that, then I'll consider taking the case."

"I'll find something," I said.

CHAPTER 31

"You're not going to believe who my new pen pal is," said Horton.

"Well?"

"Lenny 'the Mop.' You remember him?"

"How do you forget a guy who beats you at pool using the spine of a book?"

"He saw an article, of course, and wrote me. Now we're writing back and forth."

"That's great."

"Maybe," said Horton. "His marriage is in trouble again. Oh, well. It gives me a rock to push."

"What's that mean?"

"It means Camus believed the glory of being human was in expending all of our energy and effort in order to accomplish nothing," said Horton.

"Oh, like a showrunner?"

"More like rolling a rock up a hill because it gives you something to do."

"Right, like a showrunner."

Horton wasn't having any of it. Prison is not a place for humor, which to me makes the case it's the place that needs it the most. Historically, humor has thrived the most in subjugated groups, which is why you won't find any funny Nazis.

"I just don't want you wasting your time," said Horton.

"Wasting my time? Are you kidding me? It's your life we're talking about here."

Despite his pessimism, I wanted to move forward and discuss his case because, truth be told, Mary Alena's list haunted me a little. A slight haunting, but still, the only ghost I like having around is the Holy One.

"So, you think he intended to kill you both from the outset?" I asked.

"Yes. I think he was going to make himself the hero. Leaving all that circumstantial evidence? I think he was going to explain things in much the same way I did. He planned on killing me, saying he jumped me after I shot her. I'm convinced he was going to kill her either way. But his plan was to blame it on me."

"Why do you think he called 911 when he did, instead of waiting until after he killed you?"

"You know Franky better than I do, but the thing that made him a great assistant was his attention to detail. He always covered the 'what if something goes wrong' aspect of things. He couldn't call 911 afterward if he didn't survive. I think he called beforehand as a precautionary measure."

"That is basically what I told Mary Alena. So, now, is there anything you can think of that might put a crack in the evidence against you?"

"We've gone over everything I can think of," said Horton. "On paper, anyway."

"Maybe I should drive out to the scene and walk through it."

"It'll give you something to do, anyway."

"All right," I said, ignoring his Camus-inspired disposition, "we have a plan."

"You know what's the worst about being here?" he said. "I only believe in life before death."

"That's cute," I said. "Of course, death is the great tiebreaker."

He shrugged his shoulders and said, "I am trying to reason myself into the possibility that I could spend the rest of my life here."

"Why?"

"Intellectually, I have to face my own presuppositions about life that there is no such thing as meaningful justice. Sure, there is a humanly imposed justice of a sort; but since there is no God, there is no true justice. So, what do I have to complain about really? Someone beat me at a game. That's all. He made me face myself."

"The game's not over," I said. "Don't let your natural pessimism defeat you."

"Well, besides Pam, you're the only person fighting for my release. But I'm not even sure you should."

"How's that?"

"I killed Franky."

"Not in cold blood. You were trying to save your life."

"I don't know anymore," said Horton. "It happened in a millisecond; but when I had the gun on Franky, I could have yelled for him not to move. I could've given him fair warning. Maybe. Something—anything—other than shooting him."

"That's an unfair evaluation. We don't know how we'll react when our life's being threatened. We can agree on this. There is a survival instinct in the human soul."

"Still. It feels . . . I feel like I killed him."

"Well, you did kill him. But only because of circumstances."

"I dunno."

"Fine," I said. "Have reasonable doubt. But realize that's not what makes you guilty."

"No," said Horton. "Shooting him makes me guilty."

"Franky brought this on. Not you."

"I can't even give you that. It was my book. My book brought it on."

"And J.D. Salinger was guilty of killing John Lennon. C'mon," I said.

"It's not the same," he said with an unexpected degree of protestation in his voice. "People want complete moral liberation. I provided the arguments for it. Franky just applied it in a way that surprised me."

"What did you expect?"

"I mostly expected the well-educated and rich to justify their sexual behavior with it."

"You can go ahead and call them elites," I said. "It won't make you a conservative."

He nodded his head back and slightly smiled. "Got it."

This realization of his—that destroying morality comes with moral responsibility—was spiritual progress for Horton; but I didn't say anything to him, just mentally noted it to myself.

"There has to be something to tip this case," I said. "A crack somewhere."

"That's what I like about you, Sam. You believe the truth wins out."

"Well, it does."

"Not in my world," he said.

Though I find atheistic arguments for morality, reason, and justice unconvincing, I did find something Mary Alena said more compelling than anything I read in Horton's book. *Maybe Mary Alena should get a book deal,* I thought. Even though I believe God works all things according to His purposes, it was still surprising to me when Mary Alena basically told me God has a purpose for atheists in our world.

She said to me, "We (atheists) don't organize against astrologers because they're silly. Here's the thing. If all Christians were kind, we wouldn't organize. Atheists have the job of civilizing the Christians. The late comedian Steve Allen said that. And a theologian confirmed it. I went to a "Religion in Public Life" seminar a few years back and heard Methodist theologian Martin Marty speak. He said this, and I wrote it down; so the quote is accurate: 'It's the role of unbelievers to force religions to be benign.'"

It's the same idea that has been spouted by tent revivalists for generations: "the world stands in judgment of the Church." If our lives do not reflect well upon the God we serve, a group of unbelievers somewhere will surely let us know. It appears that, in a sense, atheists and prophets have similar roles.

Without even knowing it, Mary Alena actually had a good answer to the question, "What's the most positive thing atheism has contributed to the world?" Someone should pass that on to Penn & Teller.

Horton had a good law firm handle his case, but neither one of us was convinced they were positive of his innocence. They did their job. They just didn't do it with a fight. His lead attorney, Gilbert Koch, said to me during the trial, "I find all these emails troubling."

One of the most damning was this:

Franky,

One day, I'll prove to you I stand by my philosophy that nothing is wrong. But I wouldn't look forward to that day if I were you. Because you have my promise, when I prove it, I'll take you with me.

HM

Honestly, that one gave me some pause, too. But I suspected there must be something more to it. The email exchanges between Horton and Franky didn't ring true to me. They didn't sound like Horton, other than little phrases he used like, "I stand by my philosophy." But he's said that more than once in conversation and interviews, not to mention his published works.

Oddly enough, my one ally in all this, besides Pam, was Aaron Belle, the sometimes-sober *Rolling Stone* journalist.

CHAPTER 32

Aaron had become skeptical of Franky when he learned Franky acted as Horton's assistant pro bono. Aaron was skeptical by nature, but he always seemed to be skeptical of just the right things before anyone else raised their eyebrows.

He said to me, "People doing things for free makes me question their motives. Plus, I know people can get the wrong idea about Horton's viewpoint, which clearly Franky did."

But I argued that Franky got it exactly right, and that's what was hard for people like Aaron to face. Still, that didn't change the fact I wanted Horton to be innocent.

When I told Aaron I was going to drive out to the Los Angeles Rail Yard and visit the scene of the crime and think it through, he decided to ride along. Aaron referred to himself as a leaky atheist, meaning he drove a 1969 Volkswagen Beetle and only prayed when it broke down, which was never.

Aaron informed me that his Volkswagen, though in pristine condition externally, didn't have heat; so I offered to pick him up, much to his relief because it was an unusually cold day for southern California. Aaron questioned the existence of God, but he still believed in heat.

The location of the crime scene at the Los Angeles Rail Yard was in a section of abandoned rigs—much like a ghost town of decrepit trailers and rusty boxcars with this particular navy one at the end. Weeds had grown between the tracks, giving the illusion the boxcar was sitting in a garden of horsetails. Then there was the graffiti. Blue, purple, and green spray paint spelled out what looked like the word SABS near the bottom of the car; but it was so stylized, it was difficult to read. It all sat in a craggy asphalt field, so we pulled up right next to it. It was definitely a good place to commit a crime because not a soul bothered us or questioned us the entire time we were there.

I had jotted down an outline of events according to Horton's testimony. Whether he or Franky instigated the tragedy, the details would pretty much be the same, even if the villains were switched.

Resigning myself to dirty hands, I climbed up into the boxcar and extended my now grimy palm to help Aaron's normally sedentary body bend more than it had in years. He huffed and puffed for a minute before facing the direction where Miriam had been tied up.

"So, he brings Miriam in first and ties her up," I said. "And if the prosecutors are right and Franky is the one who claimed he needed privacy to rape Miriam, that's when Horton left the car, closed the door, and Franky called the police and left his whispering message."

As I verbalized these events, Aaron and I slowly walked through them, Aaron mimicking Franky's alleged movements and I Horton's. During the pivotal moment of Franky's call to the police, Aaron took out his cell phone.

"Hold everything," he said, looking at his cell.

"What?"

"I got no signal."

We looked up at a thick steel ceiling.

I pulled out my cell and reported, "Me neither. Who's your provider?"

"Sprint."

"I'm AT&T."

Then Aaron circled around the remaining space of the boxcar while looking at his cell.

"Still nothing," he said. "Do you have a transcript of Franky's call?"

"In the car."

After we climbed down and waited for Aaron to regain his breath, I read the transcript of Franky's 911 call aloud.

Operator: *911, what's the address of the emergency?*

Caller: *I only have a moment. Please listen. We're being held at gunpoint in a boxcar.*

Operator: *Give me the address.*

Caller: *Somewhere at the LA Rails.*

Operator: *The Los Angeles Rail Yard?*

Caller: *Yeah. We're inside a boxcar. Navy. There's graffiti on it. Sabo or something. Look for a Nissan Sentra. He forced me to drive here at gunpoint.*

Operator: *Someone has a firearm?*

Caller: *Horton Murray. He's forcing me to rape a woman at gunpoint. He's (inaudible) out the boxcar. Hurry. If I don't rape her, he said he'd kill me.*

Operator: *Okay, I've already got an officer searching for you. Does your car have GPS?*

Caller: *Yup, yeah.*

Operator: *Good. We can find it with that. What is your name?*

Caller: *Franky Lindgren.*

Operator: *Can you give me a number?*

Caller: *‹redacted›*

Operator: *Okay, we have two ways of tracking you. Help's on the way.*

Caller: *Hurry.*

Operator: *Help is on the way.*

"There's no way he made that call from inside this car," said Aaron.

"I think we have something here."

"Hopefully, it will cause them to look more closely at other aspects."

"I'm calling Mary Alena," I said, which I did.

She said, "Now that's something I can work with. Good job. Very good job. I'm happy to hear it. I hate injustice, and I love the chance to right a wrong. I'm just thankful his conviction has been in the last thirty days. Still, it won't be easy, but we really have something to work with here, I think."

"You think it's enough for a new trial?"

"Possibly," she said, "I have given some thought to the email exchanges between them."

"Is there a way Franky could have faked the emails?"

"Unfortunately, as I said before, they came from Murray's IP; but we can revisit everything."

"DNA and prints. You think the 911 transcript can beat those?"

"The most damning evidence is digital," she said. "On the computer. What we need is a specialist in computer forensics."

"I'll talk to Pam, his sister. I bet she'd pay for it."

"That would help."

"It's amazing to me no one investigated this aspect of things," I said. "Not his lawyers, not even the detectives."

"There was plenty of physical evidence, remember," she said.

I grunted, and she assured me that she would do her best.

During the drive back, Aaron and I discussed theism, atheism, Jesus, and the only way justice can matter. Like many atheists, Aaron was concerned about injustice. It's one of the reasons he gave for his atheism, leaky as it was.

"Justice is only reasonable," he said.

"The idea that justice is reasonable from an atheistic standpoint doesn't hold up," I said, "because the atheist gives no reason for his reason. Reason must be accounted for."

"Reason is just common sense, really," said Aaron.

"How's that?"

"Well, reason is like math. It's just another way of making calculations. It's a universal principle, really."

"Atheism assumes too much," I said. "It presupposes reason and logic as brute facts. They just exist, like mathematics. But that's not an argument. You can't just begin with reason out of nowhere. There has to be a *reason* for reason, especially if it's a universal principle. Reason can't be explained without a prior source, which would be God. Admit it. Atheism is not a big enough idea to explain reason."

"That's outrageous," he said.

"Well, you can't say it's just this principle that's just there and applies to everyone. You're giving it metaphysical qualities. Reason itself cannot hold metaphysical qualities in an atheistic worldview because the implications—like transcendence—point to the existence of God. This is why atheists must deny the truth about reason in their worldview and argue that it just works the way it does 'because of the wonderful things it does.' *Bah-dah-dah-dah-dah-dah-dah-dah,*[11] I sang out playfully. "You don't get to skip along to the Land of Oz without acknowledging that reason must have a prior source."

"Maybe," he said.

"Maybe? You are leaky."

He laughed and said, "I have to admit. That's quite an argument."

"The transcendental argument—from a debate between Christian apologist Greg Bahnsen and some atheist. You can still find it online. It's worth listening to."

"Horton's view is bleak when you think about it," he said. "I'll give you that. Depresses me."

"Then he would say you understand it."

"I guess we just make the best of what life is."

"How do you make the best of something if you don't know what it is?"

"Yeah, I hate that about you."

"Let's get something to eat," I said.

"Remember, I'm a vegetarian," he said with just a hint of self-righteousness.

---

11   *The Wizard of Oz,* Directed by Victor Fleming (1939, Beverly Hills, CA: Metro-Goldwyn-Mayer).

CHAPTER 33

I answered my cell. The voice on the other end said, "This is Penn Jillette."

"Okay," I said to give myself a moment to process what had just been said to me. "The only way I don't think this is a prank is . . . your voice is so distinct; I actually believe it's you."

"It's me," he said. "We want to pay for the forensic specialist."

Just like our last encounter, even over the phone, he could sense my confusion; so he added, "I saw Pam's post on Facebook."

"Oh, right," I said, tongue-tied amazement restricting my words.

Penn Jillette then said, "I appreciate what you're doing on his behalf."

"Thank you. We believe in his innocence."

"As do we."

So that was that. Penn & Teller financed a new investigation of technological wizards who specialized in computer forensics and could find the hidden realities in the electronic land of the dead and bring the email exchanges to life.

During their investigation, the team Penn & Teller hired— Advanced Computer Forensics—discovered that the emails from

Horton's Yahoo account, which came from his IP address, were actually sent by Franky. Thanks to our computer snoopers, it was proven that Franky downloaded Wi-Fi hacking software and then deciphered Horton's WEP encryption. It was the same with the letter detailing the crime before it happened. Franky planted it by remotely accessing Horton's desktop. That's also how he poached Horton's unpublished manuscript. Once our forensics team found a crack, it just started getting wider and wider.

The Wi-Fi hacking aspect of the case was reported by the Associated Press, and then the clincher arrived. I received a call one day from Detective Ellroy, the first detective at the scene of the crime with Officers Bellmeyer and Maxwell.

"Well, that story you planted paid off," he said.

"I didn't plant a story."

"You spearheaded the inquiry into the email exchanges."

"So?"

"So, it paid off," said Detective Ellroy. "That's what I just said. This young Marine read the story in the paper, and he called us this morning. He admitted to selling Franky the firearm."

"That's great news. I assume he's a credible witness?"

"Completely. Once the guy saw it might prove someone's innocence, he came forward. Given his demeanor, he seems a decent sort."

"Is he someone Franky knew personally?"

"Not in the least," said Detective Ellroy. "Franky found him through a website, then arranged to meet him in the parking lot of a gas station. The exchange of goods took less than five minutes."

"Is that legal?"

"Yup. He was selling one of his personal guns; and believe it or not, this was a legal sale. Background checks aren't required when a firearm is sold by a private seller, not even in California."

"This is all such great news; but I still have to ask—because it's in the back of my mind—couldn't you guys have traced the firearm?"

"Mr. Seitz," said Detective Ellroy, stuffing down his patronizing instinct as much as possible, "there is no such thing as a National Database of Firearms, so tracing guns is much more difficult than television detectives make it out to be. The guy didn't even know Franky's name but recognized his face in the paper."

"Thank goodness for that."

"So, yeah, like I said, planting that story paid off."

Later, ballistics determined the same weapon was used to kill Syd Hawkins. It's like Franky used that poor girl as a preliminary test in his "Grand Experiment" of living an authentically amoral life. Once Detective Ellroy looked into the case again, recanvassing businesses in the area of the crime, he found a gas station where one of the security cameras faced the road. (Initially, the detectives were told by the owner that the security cameras didn't work any longer, but a tech-savvy employee had fixed them one night when he was bored and neglected to tell the owner.)

It showed Franky driving by with Syd in the car the same night she was murdered. Ellroy suspected Franky had followed Syd that night. When she stopped at her new boyfriend's place, he siphoned her tank, so she would run out of gas when she left. Coincidentally, Franky would be there to pick her up. More than likely, Franky had methodically tailed her, making note of her habits. Then he had left her just enough gas to drive down the road a bit, picked her up, took her to the woods, killed her, presented it like a sex crime, took the Polaroid, and planted it in Horton's home.

As soon as I received the news about the gun sale, I drove to the Chino State Correctional Facility. It was one of those days that was so hot, the fumes on the highway looked like a gas leak spilling across the road. That, in addition to the road being full of winding zigzags, made me drive slower than usual, which was difficult because I was bursting with good news.

Before Horton even had a chance to sit down across from me, I blurted out, "We can prove Franky bought the gun."

I don't know why I expected him to be as excited about it as I was—maybe because he was the one in prison—but he only said, and without much expression, "That's good."

"That's good? It's great. He set you up. This might overturn your conviction."

He nodded and said, "We'll see," with noted indifference.

"Are you okay, man?"

"I really appreciate your friendship."

"Thanks," I said.

"But why?"

"Why what?"

"Why are you friends with me?" he asked.

Now don't think he asked this with the least bit of self-pity because he didn't. He truly wanted to know because most acquaintances had deserted him, thinking that keeping their distance was the wisest course of action. Other former friends and colleagues had publicly denounced him because it was a good opportunity to sound the alarm about a culture without values or, more specifically, with the wrong values, as everyone politicized everything to their advantage. Penn & Teller were the exception.

"I'm friends with you, first, because I like you," I said. "I think if I was an atheist, I'd believe what you believe."

"I'm glad you don't. It's a lonely belief. The way I believe it, anyway."

"What's the way you believe it?"

"There is no one to rely on. It's what defines the universe—aloneness."

"You're not suicidal, are you?"

"Only if I understand what I believe," he said and laughed. "Don't worry about me. Sincere atheism breeds despair. It was in the book."

"'Any atheist worth his salt will be suicidal.' I remember. One of my favorite quotes."

"That's sad," he said.

"It is. That's why I like it. It's only the optimistic, emotionally-based atheism people can live with."

"'The stupid intellectuals,'" he said, repeating his line. "But I'm afraid I've been the stupid one. I opened up too much of my life. I never developed serious attachments before. Everything was casual. Never had a family. Never had a serious relationship before Miriam, and it was just heading there for the first time in my life."

"I'm so sorry, man."

"Don't be. Justice doesn't exist as an absolute."

"You are depressed."

"I live with my premises. I never lived them out like Franky, but I live with them."

"No ultimate justice from which justice itself springs forth, huh?"

"That's right. And that's why I tell myself every day that I have nothing to complain about in here."

"You were set up by a crazy fanboy," I said with conviction.

"I know. And it doesn't matter."

"Well, it matters to me. And it matters to Pam. And Penn & Teller. It matters to Mary Alena, and she's gonna win your appeal."

He just looked at me and said, "Your coming here has meant a lot."

I didn't like the tense he used, but I let it pass.

"I know what it's like," I said in reference to the year or so I had spent in the slammer, but that's another story for another time.

"Not for taking another life," he said.

"No."

Then he took a long pause, examined the room for what I don't know, and said, "It felt like rape. In the boxcar. Even though I didn't rape her, it still felt that way. Because of the conditions. Her face. I could tell. It felt like rape to her. And I couldn't save her."

"You were both under duress."

"It doesn't matter. Nothing matters. And that's the end of it."

"I'm sorry, man. I'm sorry you feel that way."

"Don't say anything to Pam."

"Of course not."

"Anyway, they have a letter for you at the checkout."

"Okay," I said because I could tell that whatever it was, it was something he wanted me to read when I was alone.

Then, without looking at me or saying anything else, he just stood up and walked out of the room.

CHAPTER 34

Back in my car, I read the letter he left for me. It was handwritten because he didn't have access to a computer. This, of course, prevented him from editing his thoughts. It was the closest to Horton Murray's bare soul than anything else he'd ever written.

Sam,

As you know, prison gives you a lot of time to think. Without all the distractions of public engagements and personal interviews, I have spent too much time with myself in here. But doing so has allowed me to come to several conclusions.

First, this should come as no surprise, but I have little to no faith in the justice system. This, of course, stems from my having little to no faith in humanity and, of course, humanity living up to that assessment.

You have come closest to restoring my faith in humanity—or at least giving me a measure of it. Now, you would think I would thank you for that, but I want to give up all hope. Emotionally, I do not like what hope does to me. I don't like where it puts me internally. It's too dangerous to be up there where hope is because of what happens when it's taken away. I do not expect justice in this world, and I certainly don't expect it in death. In that sense, both emotionally and intellectually, I do live out my philosophy of life. Hope that is real and tangible just cannot exist. All hope in this world is false hope.

It's not that I don't appreciate everything you're doing on my behalf because I do. But these circumstances, beginning with Franky and his zealousness, make me want to face myself and what I write about and believe to be the case about the world; and that comes down to the fact that there is no hope. I must face the outworking of my atheism, following it to the end, even if it leads to my ruin. That's where I should have been all along. I should have faced the bleakness myself. Had I been there emotionally—in the place of accepting hopelessness—before Franky leached onto my life, I don't think things would have ended the way they did.

And I don't want you to ever feel guilty for introducing Franky to me. I have had all kinds of people try to leach onto me for all kinds of reasons. I'm the one who let Franky invade my life. You had nothing to do with that. After having a true friend, I started opening up my life. That was nothing you intended. None of it was. Things just happened. They don't mean anything, even though we want them to.

I do not want to call what happened a tragedy because like hope, nothing is really a tragedy in a meaningless universe. What I am saying is that I wouldn't have let things progress the way they did with Miriam had it not been for hope. If I hadn't been so emotionally concerned about saving her life, I might have been able to save her life. I believe my caring for her the way I did clouded my thinking, which I believe now is what got her killed. I wanted to save her, and that's where I made my mistake in handling the situation. I even promised her I would get her out of there. I gave her hope.

Her last moments were filled with a lie, and that lie was hope. I wasn't detached enough to see the situation clearly, to see a way out, to know the right move at the right time to handle Franky.

I cared too much about my own meaningless life and all the accolades and fan mail and whatnot. I liked being a celebrity author. I still do. Too much. But it bothers me to care about such things. I've never argued anything is dangerous, but my mind has changed on that account—hope is dangerous. And it was confirmed this last week.

Soon after my incarceration made national headlines, I told you I received a nice letter from Lenny "The Mop" Evans, the amazing pool shark we met in Vegas. This might not come as a surprise, but he ended up in prison, too. His first prison letter began with, "I loved my wife very much." Then one day, she broke the news to him that she was having an affair and was going to leave him. He said all he wanted to do was get her attention. He took her for a drive in the car, and sitting on the seat between them was a loaded gun. He just wanted to scare her, he said. But when she told him she had never loved him, he shot her. He wasn't thinking rationally. He reacted emotionally. I would argue that Lenny isn't your average murderer, but he became one because of what he wouldn't face. He wouldn't face the fact that his marriage had no hope left.

When he wrote to me from prison, he was tortured with guilt. Here was a man who didn't believe in God and yet felt deeply guilty for shooting his wife. As we wrote back and forth, discussing the nature of life, he began to see that his actions, though regretful to him, should not produce moral guilt in an amoral universe. I enjoyed our letters, and I think he did, too.

Then, one day, I received this short and cryptic note. All it said was, "Horton, I need to find out if there is hope or not. Lenny."

This morning, I received the news that Lenny hanged himself. He had sent me his suicide note.

One of the last things we discussed was this quote from a novel I was reading by Camus: "Men are never convinced of your reasons, of your sincerity, of the seriousness of your sufferings, except by your death. So long as you are alive, your case is doubtful; you have a right only to their skepticism."[12]

To prove he really wanted hope, he killed himself. And he convinced me—hope is dangerous. All these intangible ideas— faith, hope, love—are dangerous because they can lift you to such a place so high that when they are removed, the fall will kill you. That's why belief in God is dangerous—he's the main supplier of faith, hope, and love. And I just realized my own, never-ending hypocrisy. If nothing is wrong, then how can anything be dangerous? It's emotional. It's where I'm at emotionally and psychologically. So, I won't try to justify it.

If you can't see where this rambling letter is leading, I'm basically telling you why I don't want you to visit me anymore. You waltz in here with hope about my situation, hope about life and the future—my future—whereas I just don't think one should expect hope because it cannot exist in a universe that is alone.

You have been a good friend. No, more than that. You've been like a brother. So please look out for Pam like a brother would as I've also asked her to stop coming because this place is no place for hope.

I must stay here. On the ground. To avoid the fall.

HM

While I sat there in my car, I looked through the fence out into the prison yard and imagined Horton shuffling along in his jumpsuit—a solitary figure on the sidewalk, determined to face his philosophy of death alone. My stereo was playing a song by

---

12   Albert Camus, *The Fall* (New York City: Vintage Books, 1991).

Moby, providing an adequate soundtrack to this entire tragedy. As I listened to the song alone in my car, I wept for my friend, the image of a cloistered man pacing back and forth in his cell with Moby singing "Natural Blues" as the soundtrack to his new life.

Rubbing my eyes, I told myself I wasn't going to let Horton get away with it. I wasn't going to let him fritter away in his state of self-imposed penance, like he could pay for his own sins. I was going to prove his innocence, whether he liked it or not.

Right then, I reached over and attacked my glovebox for a pen, which I found after a violent struggle with some bothersome documents, old mechanic receipts, unapplied manuals, and once-in-a-blue-moon gadgets like a windshield ice scraper. On the back of some junk mail envelope, I leaned on the console and began composing a letter to Horton; but the pen wouldn't write at first, so I scratched it across the page until it began to bleed. All I knew was how I wanted to end it. Four lines came to me, and I didn't want to risk losing them. Believing I would finish the rest later, I wrote down my closing words right next to a block font that heralded some slogan, and I wondered if my thoughts would be as disposable to him:

We die once.
Then nothing.
Or we die once.
Then everything.

ACKNOWLEDGMENTS

I'm grateful to my friend, Marshall Allen, an author in his own right, who originally encouraged me to write my nonfiction in a narrative fashion, which became the basis of this fictional story.

Thanks to Dave Swavely, friend and editor, who helped me determine which comedic elements were too silly and just didn't fit this piece. I never thought I'd ever say it, but thanks for making me less funny. Your good questions made this a better story.

Thanks are also due to Sara Johnson, my editor at Ambassador International, who helped me finesse the closing curtain on this project. You exhibited just the right touch for a finicky writer such as myself.

There is also a slew of brilliant and godly men who receive no credit in the actual story, but their voices are there nonetheless in Sam's father and anything intelligent Sam has to say—men like Martyn Lloyd-Jones (deceased), Timothy Keller (deceased), Michael Horton (living), John Frame (living), John Piper (living), Albert Mohler (digital), and others I know I'm forgetting but will remember later and then regret forgetting.

I would like to thank Jimmy Bellmeyer who acted as my technical adviser on all police matters, which makes it sound more official than casually answering a few of my questions one Sunday morning.

Thanks to Michael Cabrera and other atheists I have known at Starbucks. Our conversations made me a better thinker—and no, it's not the caffeine speaking.

Also, thank you to Phil Courtney for taking me to a meeting of the Inland Empire Atheists, Agnostics, and Freethinkers and introducing me to a group of people who became a cast of characters in this story. If you, or they, recognize yourselves in any of these pages, it is purely coincidental, according to my lawyer.

Finally, I want to thank my wife, Dinika, who provided the details on which I based all the incidents of Sam's niece's wedding. I laughed when she told me about it, and I still laugh now. I'm especially thankful I didn't have to fly to North Carolina to experience it myself. My wife's version is probably better, anyway, because she makes everything better.

Always.

AUTHOR BIO

Thor Ramsey has written two novels, *The End Times Comedy Show* and *The Honest Atheist,* and twenty-five screenplays, two of which have been produced (*Church People* and *The Puppets of Pigeon Forge*), though he continues to have meetings. He lives with his wife and three children in Southern California and, unlike other authors, has never lived in the south of France. However, he does visit Nebraska now and then.

CONNECT WITH THOR:

www.thorramsey.com

Ambassador International's mission is to magnify the Lord Jesus Christ and promote His Gospel through the written word.

We believe through the publication of Christian literature, Jesus Christ and His Word will be exalted, believers will be strengthened in their walk with Him, and the lost will be directed to Jesus Christ as the only way of salvation.

For more information about
AMBASSADOR INTERNATIONAL
please visit:

www.ambassador-international.com

Thank you for reading this book!

*You make it possible for us to fulfill our mission,
and we are grateful for your partnership.*

*To help further our mission, please consider leaving us a review on your social media,
favorite retailer's website, Goodreads or Bookbub, or our website.*

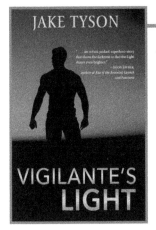

After his rescue from guerillas in Venezuela, Gideon finds himself with super-abilities, result from genetic engineering during his capture. When he returns home, he finds his beloved city in shambles and torn apart by crime. The police are understaffed and most do not care about the poor side, The Brooks. Gideon becomes a vigilante to protect his city and uses his newfound abilities. But he learns that being a vigilante comes with a price.

Betty is sure that Ida Lou does not belong in their church when the woman shows up to the Good Friday service with her small dog in tow. But before she knows what's happening, Betty—along with the other women of the WUFHs (Women United For Him)—is pushed into helping the woman. God works in mysterious ways—and through ordinary people. The town of Prosper is about to experience some drama—and it all starts with a dog who comes to church.

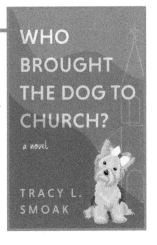

Sam Anthem has always been a team player, leading his Home Team on secret missions around the world. When he is forced on a vacation, he is introduced to a former covert ops soldier-turned pastor. But the vacation takes a turn when the Home Team comes under attack. As the team fights to stay alive against an unknown adversary, Sam begins to wonder if there is more to life than just the job. With his life on the line, Sam must decide between the job or his newfound faith and possible love.